Southern Perfection

CASEY PEELER

Southern Perfection - Second Edition- 2018
Edited by Beth Suit at BB Books
Paperback ISBN- 9780990698418
Digital ISBN- 9780990698487
Copyright © 2015 Casey Peeler

ALSO BY CASEY PEELER

For Pawpaw, thank you for always believing in me, teaching me what was right, and for never sugarcoating anything.

PROLOGUE

Raegan

Grabbing my shiny black shoes, I try to buckle them but I can't. After trying three times, I start to cry. Why do I have to wear this itchy black dress and shoes anyway? I just want to play at the barn with Cole. That's what I always do when I come to Grandaddy's, I think as the tears fall harder and I hear footsteps.

"Come here, Sunshine." Grandaddy says as he pulls me into his arms. I hug him as tight as I can. "I know this is tough, but you're a tough cookie. It's okay to be sad. I am too, but I need you to be on your best behavior today, okay?" Grandaddy says as he sits me on his knee to buckle my shoes.

Using the sleeve on my dress, I wipe my eyes and nod my head. He smiles at me. "I'm always a good girl, Grandaddy." I say proudly as we both stand and I weave my fingers in his rough hand. We make our way to his old truck and I slip getting inside with these stupid shoes. Ouch! My knee hurts! Grandaddy picks me up and checks my knee, then makes sure I get safely in my seat. When Grandaddy buckles me in, he gives me a quick kiss on the top of my head. "I love you, Grandaddy."

"I love you too, Sunshine. We're gonna get through this — me and you." I nod with a smile. He smiles back and we head to the church.

The ride to the church is short, but I keep wondering why Grandaddy said I needed to be good. I'm always good, but today I'm gonna try extra hard.

Standing at the front of the old wooden church, I am surprised by all the people. Where are they coming from? Why are they all crying? It's my mama, daddy, and grandma, not theirs. Every time I think the line is coming to an end, more people show up. Then I see Mrs. Talent, my teacher.

"Mrs. Talent! Mrs. Talent!" I say loudly, but Grandaddy takes my hand and gives it a little squeeze. Oh no! That wasn't what I was supposed to do.

Mrs. Talent bends down to me, places her hands on my arms, and begins to speak with her soft voice.

"Raegan, I'm so sorry about your parents and your grandma. The class misses you, but you take your time. Thumper, the bunny, really misses you too."

I begin to smile. I love Thumper, and he loves me, especially when I bring him an extra treat from the farm.

She stands and looks at my grandaddy. Grandaddy doesn't talk a lot, but I can tell he's sad, too.

"Mr. Lowery, we are truly sorry for your loss. Please let the school know if there is any way we can help you or Raegan."

"Mrs. Talent, thank you for everything y'all have done thus far. Raegan and I will be okay. Might take some gettin' used to, but we'll be a'ight."

Finally, I can see the end of the line. Yes! My feet hurt so bad! I'm tired and want to sit on Grandaddy's porch and let my mama read to me while we swing. Oh, wait. She can't. Thinking about her makes me sad. I miss her so much. What am I going to do without her or daddy?

As the church clears, the men in suits approach, telling us we can leave. I'm glad because they are kinda scary. Grandaddy picks me up, carries me to the truck, and buckles me in. No falling this time. The ride to the farm is quiet, except for some old music coming softly through the speakers. Grandaddy starts to sing and I try my best to act like I know the words, too.

As we turn onto the dirt road, I see my grandaddy's house, but there sure are a bunch of cars.

"Grandaddy, why are there a bunch of cars at your house?" I ask.

"Sunshine, the people from the church have brought food for us to eat. There will be a bunch of people here, but once they eat, they should go home." Good!

"Okay." I say. Be good, Rae. "Is Cole coming?" I ask.

"You bet." Grandaddy says as he gives my knee a soft pat. Yay! I get to see my cousin Cole!

Once the truck comes to a stop, I hop out and run to the porch. Where is he? I throw open the door and run into the living room to look around for Cole. Oops! There sure are a bunch of people in here. Grandaddy comes into the living room behind me, "Sunshine, he'll be here in a few minutes. Go change if you want while you wait for him."

I hurry up the steps and open my suitcase. I dig until I find my favorite shirt and shorts. I pull my dress over my head and it gets stuck on my shoulders. After a minute, I get it off and it falls onto the floor. Man that was rough! I pull on my clothes, slide on my boots, and grab my hat. This is way better!

When I get downstairs, I follow the sound of voices into the kitchen. I see Ms. Frances and a few other ladies from the church. They stop when they see me.

"Hey, Raegan!" She says too happily. "Just a few minutes and supper will be ready." Honestly, I'm not hungry. I just want to go and play.

"Okay. Thank you." I say and turn to see if Cole is here. I walk around and don't see him. Hurry up, Cole! I take a seat in my little rocking chair. I sit there like the good girl that I am. I swear I've been sitting for an hour when I hear Cole.

"Whatcha doin', Rae?" Cole says.

"Sitting and being a good girl."

He laughs. "Rae, you're always good. Come on, let's go play out back." I shake my head no. "Why not?" He says.

"Grandaddy said I had to be on my best behavior. I can't play."

Cole puts his hands in his pockets. "He didn't mean that you couldn't play. Come on." He says and pulls me by the hand. I shake my head no. "I promise, it's okay." If Cole says it's okay, I guess it is? I hop out of the rocker and we hurry out the front door.

CHAPTER 1

Twelve Years Later

Raegan

Hurrying back into the house from my morning routine on the farm, I check the clock. *Crap*. Thirty minutes to get to school. I run to my room, throw on my cheerleading uniform, slap on my makeup, and pull my long, chocolate-colored hair into a high ponytail and attach a bow the size of Texas. I double check my Vera Bradley backpack and hustle downstairs to eat breakfast with Grandaddy.

Lying on the table are fresh scrambled farm eggs, sausage, and toast with homemade pear preserves.

"Raegan, do you want coffee or tea this mornin'?" Grandaddy asks as he pours his coffee that is black as tar.

"Coffee would be great!" I say, already eating.

He makes his way to the table in his Pointer overalls, paired with a short-sleeved t-shirt. He sets down my cup and takes his seat. This has been our morning routine since I can remember, well, minus the coffee.

"How were the chickens this mornin'?"

"Same as usual. They pecked the crap outta me!"

"Ah, they're just showin' their love to ya. Was Cole already down by the barn?"

"Yeah, he was."

"I've got a lot to get done around here today, but I plan on going to the game tonight. You think you'll be home after school?"

"Of course, aren't I always? Do you care if I spend the night with Jordyn tonight?"

"I don't see why not. You deserve a night off from the farm, and don't worry about this afternoon. Cole and I will take care of it. It's a big game tonight. Now, you better take that toast to go, or you're gonna be late. I can't have that!"

"Yes, sir." Standing, I straighten my cheer skirt, and Grandaddy gives me *the look*.

"Hey, I didn't pick the length," I say as I toss up my hands.

"Well, make sure you walk close to the wall when you come down those stairs in the cross hall."

I laugh. "I can't believe we still call it that, too. Some things never change around Pleasant Hill."

After dropping my plate into the sink, I kiss him on the forehead, pick up my backpack, and walk to my truck. It's sticky hot in mid-September, so I crank up the air conditioner and the local country station. *Shoot! Ten minutes!*

Putting the pedal to the metal, I make it to school with a few minutes to spare. Everyone is still in the parking lot, taking their time getting to class. I glance in the rearview mirror for any pieces of sausage floating around before walking into the building and heading straight for my locker.

Staring into my locker, I try to pull myself together for another day at Cleveland High. Thank goodness it's Friday. I'm exhausted. I just need to make it through the game tonight, and maybe I can catch a break.

As I grab my physics textbook, my thoughts are interrupted.

"Hey, Rae! Are you ready for the game tonight?" Jordyn says bubbly.

"Yeah, Jordyn, I am."

"Are you all right? You seem a little spacey."

"Yeah, I'm just tired. You know I had to get up with the chickens this mornin'."

"I'm so glad I don't live on a farm."

"Oh, and what do you call yourself, a 'city slicker'?" I ask with a laugh.

Pleasant Hill is exactly what the name implies, a pleasant place to live that's the size of a hill. Okay, maybe I'm exaggerating just a little, but there are five thousand people in this town, tops. Most people live outside the city limits, produce their own means of food, and live like good old country folk.

When the bell rings for the end of first block, I make my way into the hall and notice Jace waiting for me. *Great! He can't take the hint. I know, the cheer captain and the quarterback are supposed to be together, but he's a true player. He only wants what he can't have. I have no time for him and his cocky-jock-self.*

"Hey, Raegan, I heard there's a party at the Phillips' farm tonight after the game. Are you goin'?" he asks.

"I'm not sure. I'm stayin' at Jordyn's tonight, so it's whatever she wants to do."

"Oh, y'all will be there," he says too confidently.

"What makes you so sure?"

He smirks and glances down the hallway to find Jordyn getting a little close to Ridge Parker.

I start to laugh and shake Jace off before heading to my next class. I'm so ready for a break, a weekend with my best friend, and just acting like a teenager instead of "Miss Perfect" all the time.

Emmett

"Hey, Jace, thanks for giving me a ride this mornin'. My truck should be fixed tomorrow."

"No problem," he says with a pat on the shoulder as I walk the halls of Cleveland High School for the first time. I can't believe I'm back in the town I never thought I'd live in again. It's the size of a peanut. "I'll catch you at the game. I think Cole's gonna get me after school."

"I wish you would have moved here two months ago, but then, I might be on the bench." Jace laughs. *Still thinking he's better than everyone. Just like the last time I was in town.*

Ignoring him, I walk into the main office, meet with the counselor, and get my schedule— calculus, physics, weight training, and AP English. *You've gotta be kiddin' me!* This schedule is no joke. I thought transferring would mean new classes, not the same ones I already had.

Shaking it off, I head down the hall and into calculus. I find a seat in the back after I introduce myself and prepare to barely pass. Who am I kidding? I'll pass, but I just want to be here, not actually have to try. The faster I can get out of this Podunk town the better, but it sure is better than living with my dad and his new wife.

When the teacher begins to speak, I realize I'm ahead of them, so I'll just listen and refresh my memory. Within minutes, my mind is wandering to the clock, the game tonight, and getting to see my stepbrother Cole. Jace is right; I should have moved here at the beginning of the summer, but I was too busy being stuck up my ex's butt.

With the sound of the bell, I make my way to physics. The hallways aren't near as crowded as my school in Georgia. Taking the schedule in my hands, I look at the room number and start to walk in that direction when I hear the sweetest and most familiar sound, but I can't place it.

Shaking it off, I round the corner to the hallway where the science rooms are located, and I hear the voice that goes with the laugh. *Who is that?* Then, I see her dark hair pulled up with an ugly bow on her head and one short uniform, talking to none other than Mr. Superstar, Jace McCoy. It takes all of two seconds for me to realize who is standing in front of me... Raegan Lowery.

Trying not to act like I see her, I make my way into the physics classroom without being noticed. Raegan Lowery is who every guy dreams about but can't have, Jace has told me this on our ride this morning. After hearing that voice, I just might have to change that.

The teacher asks me to sit up front and introduce myself to the class. *I hate being the not-so-new guy. They all know me. I've only been gone for a few years.* Once that is over, I take my seat, front and center, and get ready to learn about static electricity. The only thing I can think about is the jolt of electricity I felt when I saw her.

Raegan

Glancing at the clock, I know lunch is next on the agenda. I've got to see what the plans are for this weekend. Jordyn knows how I feel about Jace. If she's gonna be hooking up with Ridge, then I need a new game plan. With the buzz of the bell, I make my way to my locker, exchange books, and wait for Jordyn. When I see her walking down the hall, I join her.

"Hey, girl! Ridge wants me to go to the Phillips' farm. You up for it?" Taking a cleansing breath, I look at her, and she already knows what I'm thinking. "I swear, Rae. I won't leave you with him all night. I pinky promise!" she practically begs.

"Fine, but I swear, if you disappear for more than thirty seconds, I'm out!"

"Yes, Mama." She giggles.

We walk to the cafeteria and get in line. This is the best meal all week— school pizza! While Jordyn talks about her attire for tonight, all I think about is helping Grandaddy this afternoon, even if he told me I don't have to.

"I think I'm going to help Grandaddy and Cole this afternoon. I know they both wanna go to the game, and it will be faster if I help, too."

"Seriously? Why are you so responsible? I mean, you make it hard for girls like me to function in this town."

I twist my head toward her in confusion. "Huh?"

"Rae, you don't realize how much people look at you. You are the all-American Southern Belle, minus the blonde hair. You are smart, great looking, and a hard worker, no matter if it's on the farm, school, field, or whatever. The fact that you almost seem out of reach by guys doesn't help either. Like, why won't you go out with Jace? He's hot, and he's been begging for, what, like three years now?"

I stop mid-stride as she finishes her sentences. I'm speechless. I'm not that girl she's talking about. Yeah, I might look like I have it all together, but I do what has to be done in life. I will not let down my Grandaddy. He's all I have left in this world.

"Jordyn, that's so not true. I'm far from that. You know

an all-American girl has both parents to make an all-American family, and I don't."

"I didn't mean it like that. I just mean, at some point, you've got to have some fun. Ya know, hook up with a guy, go out on a date, and live a little besides a few beers every now and then."

"I just can't, and besides, Jace isn't the guy for me."

We make our way to the table. Ridge, Jace, and a few other football players are sitting together and waiting for us. Jordyn snickers as we walk over, but when my eyes land on the new guy sitting there, I can't do anything but stare.

His aqua eyes look up from his plate and meet mine. *Ohmygosh, it's Emmett Bridges. When did he move back to Pleasant Hill?* A smile widens across my face, and I'm glad he's back. He used to love to kiss us girls on the playground when we were growing up, and that's one thing I've never forgotten. What I wouldn't give to be pinned up on that playground with him right now. He's hot, but what I remember most is when my parents passed away, he brought me a stuffed bunny that looked like Thumper, our class pet. That was the day I realized everything would be okay, because I knew people cared about me. A grin escapes my lips, and as his eyes meet mine, he does the same.

Jordyn and I make our way to the table and park our trays between Ridge and Jace, like we are expected to do. Jace wastes no time introducing us to Emmett. I think he's pretty clueless to assume we don't recognize Emmett.

"Hey, Emmett, long time no see," I say sweetly.

"How are you, Raegan?" he asks with tenderness in his voice.

"Really good. How 'bout you?"

"I'm better, now," he replies. I can't help but wonder

exactly what he means by that.

Jordyn and I finish our food quickly before she asks the question I already knew was coming, and of course, it has to be in front of Jace.

"Rae, did you decide what you're going to do after school?" Jordyn questions, and for some reason, I think she's up to something.

After nodding, I fill her in, "I'm gonna help Grandaddy and Cole. I'll just meet you at your house before the game. That okay?"

"Really, Raegan? You're gonna go work on the farm before the biggest county game of the season?" Jace asks with anger in his tone.

"I hate to tell ya, Jace, but the world doesn't revolve around football. Some people have to work hard for a livin'."

With little else said, Jace makes his way outside. I swear, I don't understand him. I've told him time and time again I'm not interested.

"So, Emmett, have you seen Cole yet?" I question.

"He's supposed to pick me up today. My truck is in the shop. We're goin' to the game tonight."

As the bell rings, I stand to throw away my trash. "Ya know, I can just take ya if you want. It will save him a little time, and he might get done on the farm earlier."

"Are you sure? I mean, Jace might kill me." He smirks.

"No worries about Jace. We're *not* together." *Why did I just say that out loud? I'm sure he couldn't care less.*

"Where should I meet ya?" He says with a smirk

"I'll be out by my truck after the second bell. It's a white Chevy Silverado with my initials in teal on the back window." I say as making my way down the hall to third block.

Emmett

After class, I meet Jace in the cafeteria. I swear, school cafeterias are always the same. You have the nerds, outsiders, and popular students all separated. Once I grab my tray of food, I take a seat across from Jace. He's rambling on and on about the game. It sucks not to be playing, but I guess that's my fault. That's when I glance up mid-bite and see her talking to Jordyn. Her chocolate brown hair is pulled back so that her eyes attack you with their sharpness, but she looks upset. *Wonder what's wrong?* I try to ignore her, but I can't.

"Emmett, man, what wrong with you?" Jace asks with attitude. Then, he looks over his shoulder and sees her. "Don't even think about it."

"She's grown up... a lot," I say, and Jace smirks.

"Yeah, she has," he replies, trying to imply other things, but I know better. That's not the Raegan I knew.

As she makes her way to our table, I ignore her and wait for Jace to introduce us to boost his ego a little more. He introduces me like I'm the new kid on the block, but I'm not. She realizes what Jace is doing and lets him know that she knows exactly who I am, and that feels good to know.

While I finish my lunch, Jace gives Raegan a hard time about working on the farm. He just doesn't get it, but I guess he wouldn't, considering he hasn't had to work hard a day in his life. He doesn't deserve her, and it's obvious. That's when Raegan does the unthinkable. She gives me a means to get close to her by way of Cole. She offers to let me ride with her to the farm, and there is no way I'm not.

CHAPTER 2

Raegan

"Girl! What the heck? Jace is gonna be spittin' fire this afternoon!" Jordyn exclaims when I take my seat in English beside her.

"Really, J? I'm just taking him to Cole."

"Yeah, you keep tellin' yourself that. I saw the way you looked at him, and believe me, he noticed you long before you saw him."

"Whatever," I say as I grab my notebook and pencil.

I spend third block listening to a lot of rambling about Shakespeare and learning some stupid memory pegs. I bet I will be doing them in my sleep tonight. My last class is chorus, and it's my favorite part of the day. It doesn't take effort, and it's an escape from reality.

When the bell rings for the end of the day, I hurry to my locker and stare into it, lost in thoughts of Emmett waiting for me. Pulling myself from my thoughts, I turn and am greeted by Jace.

"Hey! Sorry, I've gotta go. I'll see ya tonight," I say leaving him standing alone. It's not that he's a bad guy; he's just not for me. Who am I kidding? He's the biggest player in school. I want someone that gets me, not what everyone thinks they know about me. I don't wanna be the cheerleader that dates the quarterback. I want to be the girl that meets a guy that loves me for my brains and beauty.

As I walk to my truck, I see Emmett propped up against it, waiting for me.

"Dang, you're fast," I say as I make my way to the driver's seat.

"Well, it looked like you were busy in there," he says as he pushes off my truck.

"He just doesn't get it, no matter how much I tell him, but don't say I said that."

He laughs. "Why not, if you've already told him?"

"Um, how long have you known Jace?"

"A long time," he adds.

"He always gets what he wants. The only reason he's still trying to talk to me is because I won't go out with him. I just don't have time for that. My grandaddy needs me too much right now."

Emmett looks at me quizzically. "What do you mean? He has Cole."

"True, but Cole doesn't live there. I've always been there to help. The work doesn't stop when the sun goes down. I help with the housework, cooking, and I'm his secretary, too."

"How do you balance it all?"

"It's pretty much all I've ever done. I don't know any different. So, when did you get into town?"

"Late last night."

"Oh, are you glad to be back?" I ask, trying to change the subject from me.

"Kinda. My stepmom is a witch. I swear, once Dad

started dating her, I knew I needed to move back in with Mom. She and George have been married for a while, and I like him. He treats her better than my dad ever did."

"That's so sweet. How is it with Cole as a brother?"

"It's okay. He's older than me, but it's good to have him around. I just can't believe that he still lives at home. That's enough about me. What've you been up to, besides the farm?"

"You know you'd live at home too if you had it made like him. Plus, I think he has no reason to leave, ya know?" Emmett nods in agreement as I think for a few seconds. "Not much more than what I said earlier. Besides school and workin' on the farm, that's about it. I have been known to throw down a little at a field party or two." I wink.

"So, does that mean you're goin' tonight?"

"Thanks to Jordyn, yes." I say a little irritated.

"Well, I'm glad," he says as he opens the truck door, and I see Cole and Grandaddy making their way to us.

Straightening my skirt, I grab my backpack and start to walk inside the house to change and work when Grandaddy stops me.

"Raegan, whatcha doin' home? I thought I told ya to have some fun," Grandaddy scorns.

I walk to him and give him a peck on the cheek. "Grandaddy, you know I couldn't do that to ya."

He looks at Cole. "What are we gonna do with her? I swear."

Cole laughs and looks at me. "Uncle Dover, I have no idea, but maybe Emmett can help us." My eyes bug outta my head. "By the way, how was your first day back, Emmett?" Cole asks, turning to Emmett.

"Okay, I guess," he says with his hands in his pockets and a shrug.

"Yeah, I bet. Come on. We're almost done; we were just fixin' the door to the barn, and then we are outta here," Cole says as he turns, and Emmett follows.

As I stand there with Grandaddy, I know he's waiting until they are out of ears' reach before he says his next words.

Before he can ask about my day, I ask him about his, "How did the appointment go?" I inquire with worry in my tone.

"Raegan, Sunshine, there's no need to worry. I'm doing fine. The doctor said it's just the old man type leukemia. I just gotta take a pill every so often. I go back next week to get it all lined up," he says with confidence and reassurance.

"Grandaddy, I don't care what they said. It's a big deal to me. I can't lose you, too!" I say as my voice heightens. He takes me and pulls me in for a hug, and I know he is strong, confident, and his positive outlook will see this through. I just know it.

"Now, listen. This is between us. Within a month or so, this should be over, and I'll be fine. Cole doesn't need any more on his plate with Emmett moving back, and I need you to focus on school and having fun. Do you understand me?"

"Yes, sir," I say as tears fill my eyes.

"Don't cry, Sunshine. I'm fine. Now, let's finish up. I wanna get a good seat for the game."

Shaking my head, I giggle. When my world stops, he makes it move again. "I'm going with you next week."

"Sunshine..." He starts to protest, but I refuse to fall to this battle.

"I'm goin'," I state forcefully as I walk into the house, slamming the screen door behind me. Rushing to my room, I change from my uniform and hurry to start supper and finish cleaning the house. *Two hours. I got this!*

I start with supper. It's got to be quick and simple. I laugh when I look inside the cabinet. I couldn't care less if I just eat a sandwich, and Grandaddy won't care either. Then, I spot a can of Beanee Weenees. That will work, and they are his favorite. Each time he fixes them, he tells me how good they are and so much better than when he was in the war. This makes me smile, and I need to smile. I need to push away what he told me. I can't lose him. I won't lose him, because I need him to survive.

After making the final decisions on supper, I head to the washroom to start the laundry. I then dust, sweep, and clean the bathrooms quickly. With just Grandaddy and me, the house stays pretty clean, except for all the hair Hank the Labrador loses. I swear, he never stops shedding. When I walk into the kitchen to warm up supper and fix a couple of sandwiches, I hear Grandaddy come inside from working.

He stops at the sink, washes his hands, and makes his way to me. "Are those Beanee Weenees I smell?" I nod yes. "Allll righhht!" he says with excitement as he rubs his hands together.

We make our plates and eat together while he asks me about my day at school, my thoughts about the game tonight, and my plans with Jordyn. "If y'all go to that field party, you be careful. You hear me?" he asks between bites.

"Yes, sir, I'll be fine. I promise there's nothing to worry about. I do have one question, though." He puts down his fork and looks at me. "Why do some guys never get the hint?"

"Whatcha mean, Sunshine?"

"Like Jace, for example. I've told him 'no' a million times, but he won't quit. I'm so tired of it."

"Raegan, you're one of a kind. He sees that. Everyone sees it, and to be perfectly honest, every guy wants what he can't have. It's as simple as that, but if he crosses any lines with you, I have a bullet with his name on it."

"Grandaddy! You wouldn't!"

"Oh, but I would. And, one more thing—be careful with Emmett."

I feel the heat in my cheeks begin to rise. "I don't know what you're talkin' 'bout," I say, trying to play dumb. *Is it that obvious he's been on my mind since I saw him in the cafeteria?*

Grandaddy looks at me like he doesn't believe me. "That boy brought you back to life with one stuffed bunny. He has no clue how that one event influenced your life, and if I was a betting man, I'd bet on the two of you. Plain and simple, but I don't want to see my Sunshine get hurt."

Without knowing what to say, I finish my sandwich and stand to clean up. Grandaddy stops me and tells me to get ready, that he will clean up tonight. I hug him and hurry to my room to change.

Opening the heavy wooden door to my room, I know my Grandaddy is right. Emmett saved me with one compassionate event. I'm sure he has no idea the impact it has had on my life, but as I walk to my bed, I pick up the stuffed bunny and hold it tightly. Not a day goes by that I don't think of him and what his innocent gift has done for me. I wipe a tear from my eye, push my parents' memory to the back of my mind, and get ready to cheer the Cleveland High varsity football team on to victory.

Emmett

As Cole and I walk farther and farther from Raegan and Mr. Lowery, I can't help but feel like I'm losing my sunshine. That's when I notice Cole laughing at me.

"What?" I question.

"I'm not sayin' a word." At that point, I grab the door to the barn and begin to help Cole. *Man, it's hot out here.* Before long, we are finished with the door, Cole puts away the tools, and we make our way to his truck. We ride to Mom's with the windows down and the local country station playing in the background.

Once we are home, Mom plays Twenty Questions about my first day back. It makes me feel good to know she's glad I'm here and not a burden. We eat supper and then get ready for the game. Football is a town event. Everyone and their mama will be there hooting and hollering for their team.

"Cole, are you goin' to the field party tonight?"

"Nah, I'm too old for that. Plus, if it gets busted, I'll be the one in trouble since I'm twenty-five. I can drop ya off, if ya like."

"Don't worry 'bout it. I'll find a ride."

"Yeah, I bet you will," he says as he elbows me.

"What's that supposed to mean?"

"Dude, you pretty much looked Rae from head to toe with Uncle Dover standing there. I don't know how you're even alive right now."

"Uhhhh," is all I can manage as the thoughts of Raegan's perfectly tanned long legs in that too short uniform enter my mind.

Cole laughs. "I'm right because you're practically doing it again. You want my advice? Not that I'm a ladies' man or anything..."

"Why not." I sit and listen to Cole. To be so young, he has the wit of an old man.

"Look, Rae is a rare gem. Girls like her are hard to find, but even harder to catch. She's lost everyone but one man in her life. I'm not sure she's ready to let him go."

"Let him go?" I question.

"Her granddaddy is her constant. I've never seen a girl so compassionate and hardworking. She puts him first, so be prepared to always come in second place."

CHAPTER 3

Raegan

"Grandaddy, I'll see ya around lunch tomorrow," I say as I kiss him goodbye at the stadium.

"Behave yourself, Sunshine, but remember to call Cole or me if you need anything."

"Yes, sir. I love you."

"Love you, too, Sunshine. Now, knock 'em dead out there." He mocks a "High V" with his best spirit fingers. *Gah! I love him!*

Grandaddy takes his reserved seat and talks to his buddies while the teams warm up. As I make my way down the stadium steps to the track, I see Jace on the field. *Why can't I be that girl? The perfect cheerleader for the perfect quarterback. It's not that I want that, but life would be so much easier.* I shake away my thoughts as Jordyn yells for me. I hurry to her on the track.

"What's up?" I ask.

"So, how did the ride home go?" she asks with her eyebrows raised.

"Wow, not beating 'round the bush, huh? It was a ride home, nothing else. I worked in the house, and he helped Cole.

They left, end of story."

"For some reason I feel like you're not tellin' me somethin'," she says. She's right, but it's not about Emmett. It's about Grandaddy.

"Nope, nothin' to tell," I say as I brush her off.

"Come on now, Rae! That boy is smokin' hot, and the way you just offered to give him a ride means something in your world. You don't do that, but whatever."

Deciding that I can't keep this info from her, I have to let her know. "J, we were standing on the porch and I swear his eyes were boring a hole through me. I think I might have been as red as a hot tamale. I can't believe Grandaddy or Cole didn't call him out."

"I'd loved to have seen that." She snickers.

Turning my attention to the field, I see Jace looking right at me. I smile and he smiles back, making his way off the field and toward me on his way to the field house.

"Raegan, thanks for being my biggest fan, and make sure you save me a dance tonight." He winks and continues to jog to the field house. I just give him a half-smile without a reply as I call the squad to get ready for the start of the game.

At exactly seven-thirty, the Chargers make their way onto the field, the stands go crazy, and the game is underway. Friday night is the best night of the week. I enjoy every minute of cheering on my high school team while watching my grandaddy relax with his friends and smile down on me from the stands, but tonight is different.

As I look into the stands, a pair of baby blues catches my attention, followed by his sandy blonde hair that is calling for my fingers to run through it. What pulls me to him even more is the fact that Emmett knows me better than anyone else in this town, and he has been gone since seventh grade. When his eyes catch mine, I turn from him, but it's too late. He caught me, and deep down, I pray he's at that field party tonight.

***

As the fourth quarter comes to an end, we have another victory under our belt. With the sound of the buzzer, we cheer in victory before shaking the opposing team's hands. Jordyn and I turn to head back to the stands when Jace yells for me.

"Hey, Raegan, I'm lookin' forward to tonight," he says with his helmet held underneath his arm.

"Look, Jace. I'm just not interested, okay? I've tried to be nice about it, but you don't seem to get it."

A look of pure shock covers his face. "It's because of *him*, isn't it?"

"No, it's not because of *him*. I've been turning you down for what feels like an eternity. I'm not a prize you get to win. I don't have time for anyone but Grandaddy, and even if I did, it wouldn't be you."

"Raegan, when did you become so rude?"

"The day I realized the only way for me to get through that thick skull of yours was to be one." I turn and walk away.

Jordyn and I don't say much as we make our way to her car. "Um, Rae, did you forget something?" she asks.

"Crap! I left my bag in Grandaddy's truck! Will you run me by the farm?" She nods. "I guess I should just follow you to the house; that way you won't have to drive me back tomorrow."

"Okay," she says with concern etched in her voice.

Once Jordyn and I are in her car, I know I'm about to get an earful. She is trying her best to hold back, but she's about to unload on me. I can feel it.

"Rae! What happened to you back there?" she asks. I just shrug my shoulders. "Seriously! I've never seen you act that way before. You are *never* mean to anyone. What aren't you tellin' me?" she says, almost like she's hurt.

"I'm fine. I'm just so sick and tired of playing games with Jace. I want to go and do as I please without having him hit on me every time I turn around. I don't want him. I have other things to worry about."

"Like what?" she asks, trying to bait me.

"Grandaddy. He's not as young as he used to be, and I have more responsibilities than ever. Jace doesn't get that. He never will, either."

"But Emmett does?" she probes as she turns to me.

"I'm not saying that, but heck, at least he's not scared to get a little dirt on his hands."

"Just admit it, Rae. It's okay to finally find someone you like. You deserve to have a guy in your life. We both know that Jace is totally wrong for you, but Emmett, girl, he's the best thing since sliced bread in this town."

I giggle. She's totally right. "Yeah, I might like him a little, but don't you dare say anything to Ridge!" I say with my finger pointed at her.

"I pinky promise," she says as our fingers lock. "Now, let's get your stuff."

Jordyn drops me off at the house, and I hurry to Grandaddy's truck to get my things. Then, I hurry inside to tell Grandaddy why I'm back. He is sitting in the living room, waiting on *Friday Night Football* to air on the local cable channel and is startled when he hears the door slam behind me.

"Sorry, Grandaddy! I forgot my bag. I'm just gonna drive to Jordyn's, so she doesn't have to bring me back tomorrow."

"A'ight, Sunshine. Be careful and remember what I said."

"I will." I kiss his forehead and walk to the truck. As I place my bag inside, my phone chirps.

Cole: Be careful tonight. Call me if you need me.

Me: Thanks

Emmett

Cole and I take our seats in the stands behind the student section. With ten minutes to go, we sit back and watch as the team makes its way to the field house. What I wouldn't give to be playing tonight. My arm is aching to pass a football down the field into the receiver's hands for a touchdown, but I guess I'll have to wait until next year for that.

I see Jace and a few other guys that I played ball with for years, but it's what Jace does that makes the anger rise within me. He looks at me and gives me a friendly nod, but not before he smirks and makes his way to Raegan. That douche bag doesn't deserve a girl like her. I'm just glad Raegan sees through him, because not many girls around here are able to get past "Mr. Quarterback".

When I think the steam is about to blow from my ears, I feel a sense of peace looking directly through me. *Raegan.* She is staring at me, and as my eyes catch hers, she tries to act like she wasn't looking. I can only hope she decides to go to that party tonight, but I have a feeling my friendship with Jace will be short-lived.

Once the Chargers pull out another victory, Cole and I make our way to the truck. We make a stop by the convenience store for a case of beer for him before we head to the house so I can get to the party. Lucky for me, George and Mom picked up my truck after we left for the game. Now, Cole can quit giving me crap about getting a ride with Raegan, even though I'd love to be in the passenger side again watching those long legs peer underneath her short skirt as she presses in the clutch.

Cole drops me off at the house to get my truck. Undoubtedly, he has other plans tonight that involve a case of beer, friends, and probably a few of Pleasant Hill's finest girls. There's one thing about Cole; he's always had to work hard in life, except in one area—girls. For as long as I can remember, he's had the best girls in town after him, but for some reason, he just keeps them at a distance.

"Hey, Emmett, here's a couple of cold ones to take with ya."

"Thanks," I say as I reach for the beers.

"Just limit it to this, and you should be fine. I'm sure there'll be a keg, but be careful. The law will be watchin' as y'all leave tonight."

"Thanks," I say, walking toward the truck.

Backing out of the driveway, I roll down the windows and turn up the radio. I take my time getting to the farm. You never want to be one of the first people there. Before realizing where I'm going, I'm driving past the Lowery farm. Raegan's truck is missing, which makes me hit the gas pedal a little harder. I can't wait to lay my eyes on her tonight.

CHAPTER 4

Raegan

After pulling into Jordyn's driveway, I park and grab my things. I should have changed at home, but we need a little girl time before she's swept away by Ridge all night. I knock as I enter the foyer and make my way to her room.

"Hey, J!"

"Well, aren't we a little happier than when I dropped ya off?" she inquires smartly.

"I'm just ready to cut loose a little."

"Awesome! I told Ridge he could just pick us up, so we wouldn't have to worry about drivin'."

Placing my hands on my hips, I turn to face her. "Really? I thought you weren't gonna be with him all night?"

"Hey, we have now and when we get back later." She smirks.

Rolling my eyes, I go to my bag and grab a pair of Daisy Duke cutoffs and a simple white tank top.

"Please, tell me you brought something other than that?" Jordyn states flatly.

"What's wrong with it?"

"Never mind." She says with an eye roll.

"No, really? Why not?"

"Rae, I know you will look perfect in that, but don't you wanna step it up a little with Emmett?"

Laughing, I then pull out what I had actually planned on wearing, a pair of cutoffs with a one-shoulder chevron tank, complemented with a pair of boots.

"Thank goodness! I was about to lose it, Rae! Not to say you couldn't pull that off. Heck, I'm sure half of the school would come dressed like that on Monday since you're the official trendsetter of Cleveland High. I want to see Jace's mouth on the ground when he realizes you were serious."

"J, it's not about Jace or Emmett; it's about me. I just want to have no worries for tonight. Did you get our drinks?"

She grins, and I know her older brother has come through, yet again. That's why Ridge is driving. He barely drinks, and if he decides to tonight, we can always call Cole to pick us up.

"I think it's time to get tipsy and do some tailgate kissin'. Whatcha think, Rae?"

"I think that sounds like a perfect plan to me," I say as I put the finishing touches on my makeup. Within twenty minutes, Ridge has arrived, and we are on our way to the Phillips' farm.

Stepping out of Ridge's Chevy with a lift kit, I take my time getting down, brush my hair with my fingers to remove the windblown look, and partake in a little shine.

"Is that one pink lemonade?" I ask Jordyn.

"Yup! It's sooooo good! But, go easy, Rae. That stuff will bite you in the rear if you're not careful."

"Thanks for lookin' out for me," I say as I take a deep gulp of the chilled liquid that quenches my thirst, hoping it hides the emotions that are lying underneath. My luck, I'll be a crying mess by the time the night is over. This charade with Grandaddy has just begun, and I already feel like I'm drowning.

"Dang! Raegan, slow down, or I'm gonna be carrying your butt back to the truck before the party starts," Ridge says with sarcasm.

"I got it. No worries," I say as I place the lid back on top of the jar and pass it to Jordyn as we walk toward the fire.

As we make our way through the moonlit field, I smile as the sound of country music fill my ears, along with the laughter of people who are now coming into view. It's time to put on my game face and be that all-American Southern Belle they claim me to be.

I see the football team near Jace's Jeep and give a friendly wave as we approach them. As Jace turns around, my eyes meet his, and I see the pleading look in them. *Does he want me to continue this game? Make him look like the guy he wants them to think he is, instead of the arrogant jerk I told off at the game?* Looking toward Jordyn, I try my best to get her to move toward another crowd, but I know it's hopeless with Ridge by her side.

"Hey, Jace," I say pleasantly.

"Hey, Raegan, are you coming to tell me you've saved me a dance?" Rather than answering out loud, I let my eyes do the talking. "A'ight, I see how it is." He laughs. *Still cocky in front of his friends, which is exactly why there is no us.*

Not wasting another minute, I grab the jar from Jordyn, take another large gulp, and lick my lips to get the last drop. As I begin to notice our surroundings, I smile when I see Emmett staring directly at me. Instead of breaking our stare like at the game, I hold it until he makes his way toward me. My soul begins to tingle, and it's *not* from the shine.

Keeping the jar in my right hand, I take a few strides toward him.

"You sure that stuff's a good idea?" Emmett asks.

"It's the best idea Jordyn's had all night," I reply in my sweetest voice.

"Look, I don't know how you usually roll 'round here, but Cole is going to party elsewhere tonight. So, if he's your ride home tonight, you might want to rethink your plan."

"That's sweet of you to worry about me, but I guess it's a good thing Ridge doesn't drink. You wanna sip?" I say, as I bat my eyelashes.

"Nah, I'm good. I have a beer, but thanks," he says before taking a swig.

I stand there like I should say something else to him, but I'm clueless. As I turn to walk back toward Jordyn, I hear his deep, rich voice. "Rae, if things get outta hand, I'll be glad to take you home tonight." *I think I like the sound of that!*

I stop mid-stride and look over my shoulder. "Thanks." I smile and walk back toward the crowd, when really all I want to do is get lost in those perfectly chiseled arms.

Once I reach Jordyn, I pass the jar back to her. I'm done for the night. No matter how much I would love to lose myself in a bottle of shine, I know tonight's not the night.

Emmett

As I approach the Phillips' farm, I notice there aren't many people around. Then, I realize that only cars are parked near the road. Not thinking too much about it, I continue driving up the dirt road until it becomes obvious why the cars are parked below. The dips and valleys in the road, along with the steep incline, make it impossible for anything without four-wheel drive to make it. I stop my truck, lock the wheels into four-wheel drive, and then slowly make my way to the party.

As my truck reaches the peak of the road, I hear the sounds of country music and people talking. I'm glad to know I'm not the first one here. Once the ground begins to level, I see a huge bonfire, trucks everywhere, and a small log cabin at the edge of the woods. This honestly has to be the best place for a party, ever. There's no way the cops can make it up here, but I'm sure they'll be waiting as we leave.

I park my truck alongside some of the others and take the beers with me as I sit on the tailgate. My eyes scan the crowd for the girl with chocolate hair and long, perfectly sculpted legs, but I don't see her. Taking a beer, I pop the top and try to relax while I wait for "Miss Southern Perfection" to arrive, because those are the textbook words to describe Raegan Lowery.

To my right, I notice Jace and some of the team have arrived. I toss my head back in a friendly nod as he makes his way over.

"What'd you think about that seventy-yard pass straight to the end zone?"

"Not as good as what I'd done, but it was a'ight," I say without a care as I take another swig of my beer.

"I guess I'll just have to wait around until next year to find out."

"Yeah, I guess."

"Cole didn't come with ya?" I shake my head no. "Too bad, I hate you're gonna have to leave here alone tonight." He laughs, and I realize the more and more I see of Jace, the less and less I want to call him my friend.

I take another long pull on my beer and try to ignore Jace, as headlights appear on the horizon. *Ridge.* Knowing there's a possibility of Raegan, I try my best to get rid of Jace.

That's a losing battle, because he's thinking exactly what I'm thinking.

Jace removes the beer from his mouth, and I wait for him to make some smart comment, just like any prick would do to stake claim on something that has never been his.

"I don't know what crawled up her butt today at the game, but she basically told me to go to away and never look her way again," he says with irritation in his voice.

I spew the contents from my mouth. *That wasn't what I thought he'd say.* "Sorry, man, I just wasn't expectin' that."

"Yeah, me either. I don't know what it is about that girl, but she's got my mind all messed up. Man, I sound like a girl, don't I?" he questions, and I smile. "Just forget this even happened. She's gonna come 'round. Once she gets a little taste, she won't be able to stop."

"Dude, don't talk about her like she's a piece of meat. She's a good girl and way too good for you."

Jace looks at me as he tightens the grip on his can while stepping forward. "You listen, Emmett. She's gonna be with me one day, and you better not try to get in the way."

I ignore him and push myself off the tailgate as I make my way to the other guys from the team, but that's not before the back passenger side door of Ridge's truck opens, and I see flawless, sun-kissed legs exiting, and I know exactly who has arrived. The question is, will she even realize I'm around?

Watching Raegan walk toward the fire is like watching a swimsuit model run down the beach in slow motion. Her legs move with ease as her long chocolate hair waves behind her. Shaking my head, I try to get her out of my mind, but it is no use, especially with her right in front of me. Too bad she walks up to Jace instead of me, but the look in his eyes shows defeat rather than victory. I know it's my time to move, but I'm frozen as I watch those perfectly voluptuous lips press against that jar, and I have to take a minute to adjust myself.

Once her eyes fall upon mine again, I make her hold her stare until I can't stand it any longer. There is no doubt she feels what I feel, but it's a matter of whether or not she acts on it. I don't do well with coming in second place. I never have and never will.

I stand confidently and make my way to her, but I'm surprised when she meets me in the middle. I decide a warning about Cole is what she needs, because quite honestly, I want her to keep her head clear and away from Jace.

Before I can control what's happening, she turns to leave. I do the only thing that feels right. I offer to give her a ride, just like she did me. Hopefully, she sees it as an opportunity like I did, but at this point, I'm unsure.

I retreat to my truck for another beer as I watch her give Jordyn the jar. *Interesting. She's quit drinking. Either she feels guilty or there is a reason she doesn't want the drunken truth to come out.*

Over the next few minutes, I watch her make her way around to all the different groups of people. She is honestly the most breathtaking creature I've ever seen, but the fact she cares about everyone is beyond hot. It's almost as if she knows all eyes are focused on her; she knows her reputation, her expectations, and it's almost routine.

With each group of people, she gets closer to me. The thought of going to talk to some guys has now fled my brain. There's no way I'm skipping a little one-on-one with Raegan Lowery.

"Hey, Raegan," I say.

"Hey, havin' fun yet?" she asks.

"Tons," I say sarcastically. "It's a lot better, now," I

answer with a half-smile.

"Emmett Bridges! Are you flirting with me?" she asks as she crosses her arms.

"Nah, I'm just stating the obvious."

"Whatever," she says as she hops up on the tailgate.

Man, this night is about to get interesting.

CHAPTER 5

Raegan

It's my duty to walk around, talk to everyone, put on a smiling face, and play the role of "Miss Perfect," so I do exactly that. What I don't expect is to catch myself standing in front of Emmett Bridges, looking like he just stepped out of latest *Buckle* catalog. Yeah, we talked earlier, but now that the shine is gone from my hands and the absence of the others, I realize how beautiful he actually is. His sandy blonde hair is covered with an Atlanta Braves ball cap with the ends peeking out the sides. As he sits on the tailgate, I can see every muscle bulging from his arms as they press into the tailgate, and his chest is broad as the river. His eyes, however, are what stop me. The crystal blue not only looks like an ocean, but it also tells a story — one of need and desire.

I stop in front of him as he says, hey. This is my chance, and I have just enough liquid courage running through my veins to follow through with my craving to be close to him.

After a brief amount of small talk, I take a seat on the tailgate beside him. When the silence is too much, we begin to talk about random stuff. Then, we get quiet again as he opens another beer.

"Dang, how many did Cole give ya?" I question.

"This is the last one," he says as he grins and brings the can to his lips. As I watch those lips touch the can, my body feels like it's one hundred degrees hotter. *What's going on with me?* That's when I hear my song. The one I pray the country station plays, the one I sing to the top of my lungs, the one about the kind of guy I need in my life, and the one that makes me forget reality. I jump from the tailgate, grab Emmett by the hand, and pull him with me.

"Come on! It's my song!" I say to him with excitement in my voice. He plants his heels firmly onto the ground. As Dustin Lynch's "Where It's At" echoes through the field, I place my hands upon his chest, close my eyes, and pray the song never stops playing.

As Emmett begins to sing the lyrics, I open my eyes and look into those baby blues. He takes a step back and points his finger at me on beat motion as he sings, "Yep, yep, that's where it's at." Then, he removes his ball cap and places it upon my head as he takes me into his arms and begins to move like he's been waiting to dance with me all night. He smiles, and I know in this moment that one boy and one song have made their mark on Raegan Lowery's personal timeline.

When the chorus begins to play again, I follow right in beat with him, sway my hips a little harder, and let my shoulders fall on beat with the "Yep, yep." I turn to him, and we both sing like no one is watching, but in reality, all eyes are on us. I'm okay, though, because that's where it's at.

As the song ends, he pulls me in for a tight hug, removes his cap, places a kiss on the top of my head, and then laces his fingers in mine. Every part of my being feels like it's coming alive.

"Thank you," I say as we walk back toward the truck.

"No, thank you. If I'd known it was gonna go like that, I wouldn't have resisted," he says as his shoulder brushes into mine.

"What can I say? I can't help it when I hear a song I like. I don't care who's watchin'."

"So, you do that often?" he questions.

"What? Dance?"

"No, drag a guy off a tailgate when you hear your song." He smirks.

As the heat begins to rise in my cheeks, I respond, "Um, no, that was a first."

He takes a step toward me and places his hand upon my cheek as my rear bumps onto the tailgate. "I'm glad that was a first, and I hope there are more where that came from." He closes the distance with his full lips pressed against mine, and I let go of the responsibilities, the what-ifs, and the unknowns that have been racing through my mind since I can remember and just live in the moment.

Emmett

The last thing I expected was for Raegan to hop up on my tailgate tonight. I'd been hoping for it, but from the way everyone talked, she was like the big catfish in the pond you hear stories about, but no one can catch. For some reason, she's letting me in, and I'd be an idiot not to act on it.

The silence between us is awkward until she makes pointless conversation. What is it about girls and their rambling? I pay attention as much as possible, but it's not until she gets quiet again that my mind begins to race. Each time I look at her, I fall harder and harder for the girl I used to kiss on the playground. That's when I see a spark in her eye, and she's yanking me from my tailgate. I see the excitement in her face, and her voice confirms it. *Crap!* I'm gonna have to dance. Not that I mind it, but I really hadn't planned on drawing much attention to us, because I know come tomorrow morning, I'm going to have a not-so-friendly visitor. As quickly as the thought enters my brain, I toss it aside. I don't care about Jace.

I recognize the song within a few eight counts. As Raegan laces her hands through mine, I can't get close enough to her, so I wrap my arms around her waist and pull her flush with me. She closes her eyes and ventures to another place.

When the chorus approaches, I decide it's time to bring her back to the present. I sing each word, and her reaction is more than I could have imagined. That's when I pull out the big guns and show her why she should be here with me. As we move to the beat, I take my ball cap and place it upon her head. Maybe it's a move I shouldn't have done, because there's nothing sexier than a girl in your cap. She must be reading my mind as she begins to dance with more intensity. It takes every ounce of effort to control the reaction my body is having while she moves against me, but when she sings, I swear I've just had a glimpse of Heaven right here in front of me.

At the last beat of the song, I pull her into the tightest embrace possible, place my ball cap back upon my head, and lay a soft kiss on the top of her head. I let my lips linger as the smell of strawberries tickles my nose, and I've now found my most favorite smell in the world. Not wanting this to end, I pull her to the truck and press her fine self against my tailgate. I make my move, and I don't care if Jace is watching. I stake my claim on the only girl I've ever cared anything about, the girl that meets me in my dreams, and when my lips touch hers, I feel peace within my soul.

When our lips break apart, I look into her eyes, and she smiles.

"Raegan, can I take you out sometime?" I ask. "Like, maybe tomorrow?"

"Eager, are we?" She smirks. "I'll have to check with Grandaddy, but I think it'll be okay."

Inside I want to jump up and give a fist pump, but instead, I keep it bundled up inside and play it cool.

"A'ight, want me to just call you tomorrow?" She nods in agreement. "Well, Miss Lowery, I might need your number first."

"Oh, yeah, probably so," she says with a hint of excitement laced within her words. She tells me her number as I type it into my phone, and then I place it back into my pocket. She glances over my shoulder and searches the crowd. "I guess I better see what Jordyn's up to."

"Are you sure?" I ask and move closer to her. She tilts her head toward mine, and this time she makes the move. Her hands reach for my chest as her soft, plump lips graze mine slightly, and then she removes them.

"Yeah, I better," she says shyly, like this is something new for her.

"A'ight, let's go find 'em." I extend my hand toward hers; she glances at it, smiles, and takes it. There's no doubt when I get home, a cold shower is going to be needed.

CHAPTER 6

Raegan

As I lace my fingers within Emmett's hand, I feel my world changing. I scan the crowd for Jordyn. It doesn't take long until I find Ridge and her talking to a group of his friends. When she notices us, her eyes go directly to our hands.

"Hey, y'all," Jordyn says, but I can tell she's about to die to know what is really going on.

"Hey, Jordyn," Emmett replies.

"So, what's the deal, pickle?" I ask her.

I can tell she's continued to drink the shine by her continuous giggle. "Maybe *you* should tell me?"

"Oh, how I love you, J! Really, I just figured you were about to call it a night. Plus, I gotta be home tomorrow by lunch for work."

"Maybe thirty more minutes? I guess it's really up to Ridge," she says as she turns to him while he's talking to his buddies in the crowd. "Let me go check and see what he wants to do." Jordyn walks toward Ridge. She wraps her arms around his waist from behind. He glances over his shoulder and gives her his full attention. It's super sweet.

"Raegan, if you're ready to go, I can take ya."

"Thanks, Em, but I can't let you take me home because I'm stayin' with J, and her mama will have a fit if I come home without her."

"I guess you've got a point."

"What?" I ask.

"Em, huh?" he asks as a sexy grin escapes his lips.

"Yeah, I guess so," I say with a shrug like it's no big deal. I didn't mean to give him a nickname; it just kinda happened.

When Jordyn returns with Ridge, I know it's time to say goodnight to Emmett.

"Come on. I'll walk ya to the truck." He guides me to Ridge's truck, opens the door, and helps me inside. "I'll call ya tomorrow. Night, Raegan," he says, closing the door and making his way back to his truck.

The ride back to Jordyn's is full of her talking nonstop about anything and everything, but she absolutely can't shut up about Emmett. I keep waiting for Ridge to comment, but nothing.

Once we get back to her house, I begin to hop out to give them a little privacy when Ridge finally decides to speak. "Raegan, just be careful. Emmett seems to be a good guy, but you didn't hear Jace runnin' his mouth. He ain't gonna let this go that easy. Just be careful."

"Thanks, Ridge," I say as I make my way out of the truck. I stop on the front porch swing while I wait on Jordyn to peel her hands off Ridge.

My mind continues to drift to Em. How can one moment in time make me feel so happy or alive, even? I've lived my life like I'm supposed to. I do exactly what is expected and asked of me, but right now, I want to be selfish and keep Emmett Bridges all to myself.

The humidity from this late summer night is smoldering as I wait for Jordyn. I wish she'd come on. My phone buzzes in my hand. *Who could this be?* Glancing down, I read Emmett's name on the screen and squeal with excitement. Em.

Emmett: Just wanted to make sure you made it
to Jordyn's ok. I'll call you tomorrow.
Me: We did! K :)

My reply is simple, because I don't want him to think I'm sitting around waiting for him to call, even though I wanted to jump up and down like a crazy girl when his name lit up my screen.

Quickly, I change his contact info to "Em," and as I put away my phone, I see Jordyn making her way up the steps. "What you cheesin' 'bout?" she asks.

"Nothin'."

"Yeah, that's what I'd say, too. Come on. I want the deets!"

Jordyn and I walk inside her house and to her room. As soon as the door is shut, she starts her twenty questions.

"Girl, you need to tell me what happened out there tonight. I know you were makin' your rounds, but holy freakin' moly, you should have seen Jace's face when you started dancin' with Emmett. I thought he was gonna go over there and beat his face in."

With an eye roll, I reply, "Well, it's not like I planned it or anything. J, there's just something about him! I mean, never in my life has a guy caught my attention like him. He's sweet, and ohmygawsh, have you seen that body, not to mention those lips? I'd swear Channing Tatum with sandy blonde hair was standing in front of me!"

"I totally see Channing Tatum! Wait? Lips? What did I miss?"

"So you didn't see the kiss?" Jordyn looks at me clueless. "J, when we were dancing. As the song ended, he kissed me. Right there in front of everyone. I swear I never want anyone else to touch these lips... ever!"

Jordyn begins to giggle. "Don't you think that's a little dramatic?"

"Uh, no. Not to say I have the most experience in that area, but I know enough to know that I think I saw stars."

Jordyn takes a minute before she speaks again, "But, really, Rae, what are you gonna allow to happen between you two? I know you well enough to know your grandaddy is always first."

Grandaddy does come first, and right now, he needs me more than I need a boy.

"I need to leave Emmett alone. Grandaddy does come first."

"Aw, heck to the no! He might come first, but there's no way I'm letting you toss Emmett to the side, especially after what I just witnessed in that field."

Thinking of him perched on the tailgate makes the corners of my mouth lift, and I know she's right, but I'm going to have to keep Grandaddy first until we know what's going on.

"J, I know you're right, but Grandaddy needs me more than ever. I can't just bring someone new into my life like that."

"For cryin' out loud! He's Cole's stepbrother, and you know how much he loves Cole."

"True, but..."

"No buts! Just listen to the beat of your heart for once. That's all I'm askin'."

"Gah! A'ight! Now, I want to know about you and Ridge. I thought you weren't gonna be around him all night."

"Like you can talk. Once you sat on that tailgate, I knew I didn't have to guess where you were the remainder of the night."

Emmett

As I watch Raegan disappear into the night, I can't help but wish I were with her. As I turn, I think about walking back to the crowd, but realize that could be a mistake while Jace's eyes are on me. Instead, I give him a slight nod and make my way to my truck.

By the time the tires hit the highway, images of Raegan sitting on the bed of my truck are all I can think about. There's no way I can go to bed now. I text Cole, and he tells me where he's partying, and I go to meet him.

Once I arrive, I can't stand it any longer. I know the rule of waiting at least three days to call a girl, but I couldn't care less. I take out my phone and text her.

"What's up, man?" Cole asks as I walk to the fire pit.

"Ah, ya know. Same old field party, just a different town."

"I bet. So, why didn't you head home? You know your mama's gonna wonder."

"I don't know. She knows where I am. So how 'bout another cold one?" I ask him.

Shaking his head, he tosses me one. Then, he introduces me to the crew around the flames. I recognize a few guys, and there are three girls perched up on their laps. I take a seat beside Cole and pop a top. I listen to their conversation and put in my two cents when I can, but in reality, I'm only thinking about one thing right now—the look in Raegan Lowery's eyes when she realized I'm not like the others.

Around two in the morning, we make our way home. As we are walking toward the house, Cole finally says what he's been thinking, "I take it Rae has your mind all tore up?"

"I guess you could say that."

"Just remember what I told ya. Grandaddy comes first, but I'm tellin' ya now, if you hurt her, I'll personally make sure you pay and not think twice."

I don't say anything as we go our separate ways once we are inside the house. After making my way to my room, I decide a shower is definitely in order, because I can't focus for anything. I need to clear my mind of Raegan, but she's consuming me more and more by the minute.

CHAPTER 7

Raegan

After tossing and turning half the night, I finally drift off to sleep. I wake up to the smell of coffee and pancakes coming from the kitchen. *Yum!* I love Jordyn's mom! Throwing off the covers, I hear Jordyn grumble and roll over.

"Come on, Sleepy Head! I smell pancakes!"

"Rae! Five more minutes. That's all I want," she protests.

"Yeah, and then that turns into ten, then twenty. Come on. I gotta get goin' soon."

"Fine! But only because I love ya," she says as she throws off the covers, and we make our way down for breakfast.

"I know," I say confidently, and we eat until our bellies can't handle any more.

After breakfast, I change, get my stuff together, and tell Jordyn I'll call her later.

"Girl, you better call me! I gotta know how this date goes tonight."

"Yeah, if I go."

"Hold up! Whatcha mean?"

"Forget it."

"Like hell I will!" she exclaims, and we hear her mama yell for her to watch her mouth.

"Look, I've got some things to take care of today. I need to make sure Grandaddy doesn't need me tonight before I decide to go."

"Stop coming up with lame excuses. You like him; he likes you. Have fun."

"We'll see," I say, knowing good and well I'm going out with him tonight.

While driving to the farm, I roll down the windows and let my thoughts drift to last night. Then, thoughts of Grandaddy and my conversation with him enter my mind, and tears form in the corners of my eyes. I brush them away and turn up the radio to try to focus my thoughts on something else.

Putting the truck into park, I look in my rearview mirror to see there is no evidence of my meltdown, so I grab my bag and go inside.

"Grandaddy, I'm home!" I holler as I close the door behind me. I don't hear him, but the closer I get to the rear of the house, the clearer I hear the radio playing. Opening the door to the back porch, I see him humming along and shelling pecans from his rocking chair.

"There ya are," I say as I take a seat beside him, place an old newspaper onto my lap, and begin to shell them, too.

"Boy, they are good, ain't they?" he asks as he eats a freshly cracked pecan. I smile for assurance. "So, how was it last night?"

"Good, real good."

"Uh huh. I know you, Sunshine. Remember that. I know you don't exactly like those parties, but you go 'cause people expect it. So, spill it."

After cracking several pecans, I finally find the words to

tell Grandaddy. "I kinda told Jace McCoy off after the game."

"You're kiddin' me." He stops mid-crack. I shake my head no. "'Bout time. You know, you're more like your mawmaw than ya know. She'd tell ya exactly what she thought and wouldn't care who was around to hear it."

"Do you miss her?" I ask.

"Every day, but she's smilin' down on us. They all are; don't ever forget that, Sunshine."

"When you met Mawmaw the first time, what was it like?"

Grandaddy turns to me. "Rae, I'd known your mawmaw my entire life, but it wasn't until I was about fifteen years old that I realized there was more to her than just a girl. She was always offering to help me do my homework and bringing me fried pies. Man, they were good. One day, she finally just laid it out onto the table. She never beat 'round the bush. She pretty much asked 'are you gonna ask me on a date or what?' I knew right then she was the girl for me. She never made me guess what she was thinkin', she told it like it was, and she always let me know if she didn't like what was goin' on."

"Oh, okay," I say as I continue to crack pecans.

"What's this really 'bout?" he questions.

"I kinda think I like Emmett Bridges."

A wide grin covers my grandaddy's face. "I kinda knew that already, and you know what? I think he kinda likes you, too."

"He asked me out tonight," I say nonchalantly.

"Well, Sunshine, what'd you tell 'em?"

"That I'd have to check with you."

"What am I gonna do with you? You better go. This old man can survive a meal on his own for a night."

We both laugh, and I feel happy. Grandaddy approves,

and I have a real date tonight with *the Emmett Bridges*. That is, if he calls.

Emmett

I woke up with the chickens this morning. I tried my best to doze back off, but it was pointless. I fell asleep with the image of Raegan Lowery's eyes and woke up to them.

Needing to clear my thoughts, I go for a long run. I bypass a shirt, tossing on only shorts and running shoes. After stretching, I take off down the country back roads.

Even after almost three miles, thoughts of her still consume my brain, and that's when I notice her truck stopped at the stoplight. I run a little faster to try to get a glimpse of my southern perfection, but the closer I get, the sadder she looks. She takes her hands and wipes away what I think are tears. *What would make a beautiful girl cry? Does she regret last night? Has Jace done something?* Anger fills my veins. I don't want her to see me, so I turn and run home. I now have a decision to make. Call her or not?

Once I'm back at the house, I hurry to Cole's room. "Hey, man, you gotta minute?"

"Yeah," he says as he finishes tying his boots.

"I just saw Raegan while I was runnin'. She was cryin'. Do you know why she might be upset?"

"Dude, you got it bad. Rae's a strong girl. She doesn't bare her soul to many. I'm thinkin' she was alone and was missin' her folks. Sometimes when I'm at work, I catch her wiping away tears when she thinks she's alone. I wouldn't sweat it."

"Thanks, Cole," I say as I back out of his doorframe.

"Hey, Emmett, she likes you. Question is, does Uncle

Dover?" he says with a laugh.

"Shut up," I reply and head to take another shower.

The rest of the morning, I try to bide my time until I can call Raegan. I don't want to sound too eager, but Mom's starting to question who this boy is in her house. I've cleaned my room, pulled weeds, mowed the grass, and did my laundry.

"Emmett, are you okay?" Mom asks.

"Yeah, I'm fine. Just tryin' to stay busy."

"Are you sure?"

"Yeah."

"Okay, well, George and I are going to a fundraiser tonight. I can get you an extra ticket if you wanna join us."

"Um, I might have a date."

"Emmett James Bridges, is that why you've been workin' yourself to death this mornin'? What cute little girl has your nerves tore up?"

"Mom, it's no big deal."

"I beg to differ. You might not have been under this roof in a while, but I know you don't keep your room clean, and your daddy had to beg you to mow the grass," she says with her hands on her hips.

"Fine. Raegan Lowery," I tell her as I turn to grab my clothes from the dryer.

She follows me into the laundry room, crosses her arms, and leans against the wall. "Is there anything you want to add to that?"

"No, ma'am." After waiting about thirty seconds, she takes the hint and turns to complete a few other Saturday morning chores.

I carry my clothes to my room to fold them. When I glance at the clock, it's only twelve-fifteen. *I'll wait ten more minutes.*

CHAPTER 8

Raegan

While enjoying the warm breeze from the back porch with Grandaddy, I continue to stare at my watch.

"Sunshine, don't you know a watched pot never boils?" Grandaddy jokes.

"I know. He said he'd call after lunch, and well, it's after lunch."

Grandaddy shakes his head. "What am I gonna do with you? You gotta learn patience." We continue to shell pecans. After I get a good rhythm going, I feel my phone buzz in my pocket. I almost jump from my seat, but I try to refrain from acting too excited. *Hurry, Raegan, or it's gonna go to voicemail!* I grab it and hit *Accept*.

"Hey, Raegan, it's Emmett. Um, I was just wondering if you had time to talk to your grandaddy about tonight."

"Yeah, I can go tonight. He said it was fine," While trying to keep down my voice, I feel the excitement build within me. I have a *real* date tonight, and it's not with Jace! *Hallelujah!*

"A'ight, then I'll pick ya up 'bout six."

"I'm lookin' forward to it."

"Me, too. See ya tonight." I touch the *End* key and break out into a happy dance and a squeal in the laundry room. Once I compose myself, I walk back out toward Grandaddy, pick up my things, and continue to help him.

"That went well," he says.

As my cheeks turn about fifty shades of red, I shake my head yes. We sit on the back porch, relax, laugh, and enjoy each other's company. Grandaddy hums his favorite hymns, and I fall in sync with the words.

"Sunshine, your voice is bright as a canary."

"Well, I think I get it from you," I say.

"I know for sure it didn't come from your daddy. He couldn't carry a tune in a bucket." We both laugh.

As the afternoon rolls around, so do the chores on the farm. Grandaddy bush hogs the field while I clean out the stalls. About halfway through, I take a short break and grab a glass of water when I see Cole's truck pulling up. *I wonder what he's doin' here.* I place my glass into the sink and make my way outside to meet him.

"Cole, whatcha doin' here? You do know you're off today, right?" I ask.

"Yeah, silly girl, I do. I left my fishin' rod here last week, and I think we're going down to the pond to see if we can catch a bite for supper."

"Oh, okay. Have fun and catch a bigun for me!"

"I will. What's Uncle Dover got ya doin' now?"

"Just cleanin' out the stalls. Nothing special."

"Do you want some help?" he asks. I can tell Cole is up to something, but what, I'm not sure.

"Um, aren't you goin' fishin'?"

"In a little while. I don't mind helping you first," he states like he doesn't care about the fishing excursion.

"How 'bout you just spit out what you wanna say and mosey on?" I ask with a little attitude.

"How 'bout I work and talk at the same time?" he counters right back.

"I guess, but who wants to shovel poop on their day off? You must be crazy," I say as we make our way to the barn.

Cole removes his shirt to where his undershirt is all that remains to cover his hard as a brick body. I can't grasp why he hasn't found a girl yet. I mean, it's not like he's old, but it's almost like he couldn't care less. I push away that thought, and we get to business. After a minute or two of silence, he finally starts to talk.

"Rae, I'm just gonna lay it out there for ya."

"You know, you're kinda scarin' me," I say with a little nervousness in my voice.

"No need to be scared, but I just want you to know. I know what's going on."

"Okay… so, you know I have a date tonight with your stepbrother, no biggie." I figured he knew that already, so I have no idea why he had to come here and say it, unless there's something I don't know about Em.

He stops what he is doing, puts down the shovel, wipes his hands on his jeans, and then walks toward me with both fear and compassion in his eyes.

"I know, Rae. I know something's wrong with Uncle Dover." With those words, I drop my shovel and fall into Cole's arms. He doesn't say a word. He just lets me cry.

I finally pull myself together and away from him. "How'd you know?" I ask as I wipe my tears with the hem of my shirt. *Really ladylike, I know.*

"He had me go to the doctor with him." I begin to speak, but he stops me. "Stop, Rae. He wasn't gonna let me, but he just said he needed someone else to know that could take care of you if something happened to him."

"Why didn't he tell me you knew?" I question.

"I'm not sure. I think he just wants to act like everything's okay, and the doctor said a few pills might fix it. He knows you, Rae, and he knows you don't talk to many people. He also knows I've been around you as long as he has, so I am his best bet in case something goes wrong."

Wrong. That word hits me like a knife in the heart. "Nothin' is gonna go wrong, Cole! Grandaddy's gonna be fine. He said so. The doctor said so. We just have to keep the farm goin' and keep it to ourselves. We've already been the pity of this town when I was five, and I'm sure not gonna let that happen again!" I yell at him.

As if he knows exactly what to do, he pulls me in again. "Rae, I'm not sayin' I'm gonna announce it to the world. I just wanted you to know you have someone to talk to. I love ya. I always have. You're my cousin and I'm here for ya, okay?" he says as he lifts my chin toward him. Now, let's hurry up, so you can get ready for your date with *Emmett*," he says in his most girly voice.

I push off him and fling one shovel of manure right at him, but I play nice because it lands a couple of feet away from him.

"Girl, you better be glad that didn't land on me. I'm tryin' to help ya, for cryin' out loud."

I smirk and keep working. When we finish, I give Cole a glass of water. He gets his fishing rod, stops by to talk to Grandaddy, and then leaves. There is something about that boy that always makes me smile. I guess he is like the brother I've never had, and I am relieved the secret isn't only kept with me.

Once Cole is gone, I check to make sure Grandaddy

doesn't need anything else done around the farm. He just has to give the animals some fresh water, and he will be done, so I go inside to get ready.

Looking in my closet, I try to figure out what I'm going to wear. When nothing strikes my fancy, I decide to shower first and then find something later. I grab my iPod, turn on iTunes Radio, and crank up some good ol' country music. I spend the next hour singing, showering, dancing like a fool, and making my legs silky smooth. Then, it's time to decide what to wear. This would be so much easier if I had a clue where we were going. I don't want to dress too laid back, but I don't want to overdo it, either. I mean, we're in Pleasant Hill for goodness sake. It's not like there's much to do here.

As I begin to rummage through my closet, I find my cream colored, long-sleeved, lace top. From the front, it appears pretty plain, but when I look at the back, I know it's the one to wear. The back looks like an upside-down triangle is missing, and it shows off my back perfectly. Knowing I want to try to keep my look casual chic, I match it with my dark denim cutoffs and a pair of crocheted slouch boots. Now that this decision is made, I make my way back to the bathroom to finish my makeup and hair.

As I pause to look at my reflection, I stand silently as I see a girl who is the spitting image of her mother. I vaguely remember my mother's chocolate locks that flowed halfway down her back and how she pulled it up into a messy bun when it got hot. I'd ask her to do the same to mine, and she would. My heart hurts for her. How I wish she were here to talk to me about boys, life, and what she wants for my future. Sometimes a girl just needs her mama. I smile and speak out loud to her, "Mama, I hope I make you proud. I miss you."

I don't know if it's my subconscious or just wishful

thinking, but I can hear her saying, "You bet I am, sweet girl. Now, knock 'em dead out there." And, just like that, I feel her around me, and I know I'm going to be okay, regardless of what the future holds.

Looking at my watch, I realize it's almost time for Emmett to arrive. I take a little product and run it through my hair to help with the frizz that will happen later from the Carolina humidity. I grab my accessories, change my purse to match, and make my way down the hallway to talk with Grandaddy until Emmett gets here.

Grandaddy is sitting in the kitchen, reading the newest *Our State* magazine as I enter. He looks up, and I know words are coming. I brace myself.

"Sunshine, you look beautiful. Emmett is one lucky boy, but I got my shotgun ready to scare him a little."

"Grandaddy!" I exclaim.

"Hey, you got to let those boys know we mean business, even if he is a good guy. They are only out for one thing, no matter what they tell ya. I was young once, too, ya know?"

"Whatcha talkin' 'bout? You're still young," I say as I give him a hug.

"That's my girl. Makin' your old man feel good," he says with a laugh. "But, listen to me, Rae. I know you're excited, and you look like a million bucks, but be careful. I'd hate to have to whoop that poor boy over you."

Gasping, I say, "Such language."

"Hey, I'm just tryin' to get my point across. Really, be careful, have fun, and don't do anything I wouldn't do," he says, as there is a light knock on the door. "Oh, let me," he suggests with a shrewd grin. Grandaddy stands from the table, grabs his shotgun from the corner, and heads for the front door. *Oh, gawsh! I wanna die from embarrassment!* I put on a smile and wait for Emmett's reaction. Grandaddy opens the door with the gun in his hand.

"Good evening, Mr. Lowery," Emmett says calmly, but the expression on his face looks like he's ready to about-face and run as I peek around the kitchen corner.

"Emmett, come in," Grandaddy says flatly, and I try to resist the urge to giggle. They make their way into the foyer. "Rae will be out in just a minute, but I wanted to talk to you first."

"Yes, sir," Emmett replies.

"I expect you to take care of her, Emmett Bridges. She's a good girl, and I love her more than life itself. If you hurt her, by God, I'll make you wish you never stepped foot back into Pleasant Hill. Got it?"

"Yes, sir."

"A'ight. Now, have her home by eleven."

"Will do, Mr. Lowery."

"Sunshine!" Grandaddy hollers. "Emmett's here."

On that cue, I walk into the foyer to meet him. When I round the corner, I see him standing there in a pair of jeans and a fitted polo, holding a bouquet of daisies. I feel as if the world stops spinning when I see him. A smile spreads across his face, but I can see he's trying to refrain from a real reaction with Grandaddy standing there.

"You look gorgeous, Raegan," Emmett states as his smile continues to grow.

"Thanks," I respond as he hands me the flowers. "They're beautiful; let me put them in some water real quick."

As I start to make my way toward the kitchen, Grandaddy intercepts me. "I'll take 'em. You two go on."

"Thanks, Grandaddy. I love you," I say as I give him the flowers and a kiss on the cheek.

"Love you, too."

With that, Emmett and I make our way out the door toward his truck.

Emmett

After hanging up the phone, I throw it onto the bed. Now, what to do to kill time until our date. I just might take a ride to see exactly what we can do tonight. I'm thinking she's more than a dinner and movie kinda girl, but what?

I walk into my room and grab my phone, keys, and ball cap as Mom yells for me. "Yeah?" I answer.

"Did you talk to her yet?" she asks.

"Yes, ma'am, I'm pickin' her up at six, but I have no clue where to take her."

Mom ponders a moment, and then her face lights up. "I heard there's a band playing at The Shed tonight. That might be fun, and maybe take her somewhere nice to eat, like Smoke?"

"Thanks, Mom, I actually kinda like those ideas."

"You're welcome. Just be home by midnight."

"Yes, ma'am." I scratch the idea of a ride and decide to hang around the house. As I walk to the barn, I pass Cole who is obviously looking for something. His fishing pole of course, and it's at the Lowery Farm. Shaking my head, I pull the cover off the four-wheeler and make my way to the woods out back.

After riding around for an hour or so, I return to the house to get ready for the night. Not that it will take long, but the sooner six o'clock gets here, the better.

Cole's truck is gone when I get back to the house. I wonder if he got to see her, and a hint of jealousy races through my veins. I shake it from my head and go inside. I hurry upstairs to shower and get dressed.

Once I'm ready, I turn on ESPN and relax for a little while. That's when the idea hits me. *Flowers! I need flowers!* Looking at the clock, I have more than enough time to go and buy her some at the farmers' market. Grabbing my things, I let Mom know I'm leaving and make my way there.

As I pull into the farmers' market, the crowds are leaving and the vendors are packing up for the day. I hope I'm not too late. Glancing around, I see a guy loading up flowers onto a truck to head back home. I make my way toward him.

"Excuse me, sir. Do you have time to sell one more set?" I say.

"I just might. Who's the lucky lady?" he asks.

"Her name's Raegan."

He smiles a little wider. "As in Raegan Lowery?"

"Yes, sir."

"She's one of the sweetest girls I know. You take your pick. They're on me," he says as he continues to load baskets.

"Thanks," I respond as I begin to look through the baskets. It doesn't take long for me to decide on a bouquet of daisies. They are beautiful, simple, and remind me of Raegan. "I'll take these. Are you sure I don't owe ya anything?"

"Nope," he replies, and I try to give him some money, but he refuses.

"Thank you, sir," I say and make my way back to my truck. I make one stop for gas and then head to the Lowery farm. As I pull down the driveway, I try to push my nerves to the side.

Once I arrive at the farm, I walk to the front porch, take a deep breath, and knock on the door. Then, I wait for what feels like an eternity until I come face-to-face with Mr. Lowery and his shotgun. *Pull yourself together.*

CHAPTER 9

Raegan

As we make our way to his truck, Emmett's hand skims my back and goose bumps rise all over my body. I try my best not to react the way I'd really like to. He opens the door and helps me inside before making his way to the driver's side.

He places the key into the ignition, turns to me, and smiles as we make our way to dinner. The truck is quiet while Emmett drives, as if neither of us knows what to say.

"So, Em, you gonna let me in on our plans tonight?" I ask.

His eyes meet mine in a glance. "I guess I could. I was thinkin' 'bout goin' to eat at Smoke and then maybe checkin' out the band at The Shed."

I ponder the idea for a moment, and all I can think about is the way our bodies moved together the last time we danced, so I'm definitely in on this idea of a date. "I think I like that idea, especially the last part," I say as a wide grin escapes my lips.

"Oh, do ya now?" he questions.

"Yup," I answer as he takes my hand in his and laces our fingers together.

Within minutes, we are at Smoke. For our quaint, little town, Smoke is the place to go for something Southern yet classy. As we enter the restaurant, the smells of Southern fried foods tickle my nose, and I can't wait to dig into those fried pickles.

The hostess takes us to a table near the middle of the restaurant. Emmett pulls out my chair for me before taking a seat, and the hostess gives us a rundown on the specials for the evening.

After the waitress introduces herself and gets our drink order, we scan the menu.

"Raegan, do you want an appetizer?" Emmett asks.

"Fried pickles?" I scrunch up my nose and request with a little hesitation.

He takes his hand and throws it over his heart. "Oh gosh, I think you just stole it." I burst out laughing. "Please, tell me you're not ordering fried mac-n-cheese? If so, go ahead and call the morgue!"

"No, I'm not ordering fried mac-n-cheese, so I think you're safe," I say with a wink.

We order and then enjoy each other's company before our food arrives.

"You know what, Raegan?" Looking up mid-bite, I finish chewing before placing my fork onto the table. "You are, by far, the most beautiful girl I've ever met." It was a good thing I'd already swallowed my food, or I would have choked!

"Em, I'm sure that's not the case."

"Don't kid yourself, Rae. I can still remember what you looked like when we were kids, and even though I didn't want anything to do with girls, I knew there was something special about you."

"Um, Em, I hate to break it to you, but you used to kiss

me and every other girl on the playground, so I'm pretty sure you wanted something to do with us." His face turns bright red. "Ohmygosh, is Emmett Bridges embarrassed?" He shakes his head. Leaning a little closer to the table, I whisper to him, "I gotta secret. Seein' ya this way is kinda hot." I lean back in my chair and wait for his reaction. Never, ever, do I just lay words on the table like that.

"Well, honey, I'll turn as red as a tomato if it keeps you usin' words like that." He sits back and crosses his arms. This is going to be an interesting night.

Emmett

Once we finish eating, I pay, and we make our way to my truck. The way she took my comment so lightly, like she isn't that pretty, really bothers me. She's got to know she's more than just looks in my book, and I'm 'bout to tell her.

"I meant what I said in the restaurant, Raegan. You are the smartest, hardest working, most beautiful, and most caring Southern Belle I've ever met. Don't ever sell yourself short." I stare into her eyes, and place one small, but monumental, kiss on her perfectly plump lips. It's times like these I wish I had a bench seat instead of captain's chairs. When I pull away, she gasps, and I know she feels exactly what I do. I place the truck into reverse before we make our way to The Shed.

During the drive to The Shed, she looks at me and smiles as we listen to the radio. She begins to sweetly sing the harmony to Blake Shelton's "My Eyes," and in that moment, my life changes for the better.

"Raegan, I knew you could sing, but, man." She just shrugs her shoulders. "Really, Rae, you need to give yourself more credit."

"It's no biggie, but I get it from my grandaddy."

"It is a big deal. Can I ask you something, and you promise not to take it the wrong way?"

"Sure."

"Why do you feel like you have to be the girl that everyone expects you to be?" I ask as I approach a stoplight. She stops, takes a moment before she speaks, and then says the most honest words I've ever heard.

"Em, over the years, the farm and its responsibilities have grown, and people have come to expect certain things from me. I'm not perfect by any means, but I don't want to let anyone down, especially Grandaddy. Since I can remember, I've done everything he's asked and I'd hate to disappoint him. In my life, I've lost a lot, but I'm also thankful for the support I've had over the years. That's why I do the things I do. I do what is expected, and I do what's right."

"Do you ever get tired of it all?"

"Sometimes, but that's our secret."

I smile as the light changes.

"Em, wanna know another one?" she questions.

"Shoot," I reply.

"For some reason, I feel like I can just be me with you. Not the all-American perfect student, cheer captain, granddaughter, or anything. Just plain ol' Rae."

I don't exactly know what to say to that, so I do what any other guy would do. I reply as simple as possible, "I'm glad." I squeeze her hand a little tighter.

Before long, we are pulling into The Shed. The parking lot is beginning to fill up. I'm not sure which band is playing tonight, but from what I've heard, they're all great.

I hurry around to let Raegan out of the truck. She slides down and turns to grab her purse. I shut my eyes to try to keep the excitement from building as her gorgeous figure turns around and leans into the cab of my truck. Then, she turns to face me.

"Em, are you okay?" she asks.

Knowing I just got caught, I smile. "Yeah, everything is perfect." She grabs my hand, and we walk to the door.

Pushing open the wooden door, we make our way to the cashier, who is around sixty, but trying to live like she's still twenty-two. Smacking her gum, she looks at us.

"Two?" she asks for reassurance.

"Yes, ma'am," I say as I let go of Raegan's hand to grab my wallet.

"That'll be ten dollars, Hot Stuff," she says with a wink.

After paying, Raegan takes my hand in hers. "Come on, Hot Stuff!" I just shake my head.

As we enter the main area, the lights are dimly lit with some type of string lights, people are sitting at tables, the band members look as if they are about to start playing, and several couples are already on the dance floor as the stereo blasts country music through the speakers. I guide Raegan toward a small table off to the side, and we take a seat.

"Have you heard of them?" I ask her as I point toward the band.

"Yeah, do you see that drummer right there?" I nod. "That's Bobby Parker. He's about Cole's age and goes to church with us. You'll see him in the mornin'."

"You're kiddin' me, right?" I ask.

"Nope. You know as well as I do, people down South go to a good honky tonk on Saturday night and church on Sunday mornin'."

I stop and think about it, realizing she's telling the truth. "Yeah, it's the same in Georgia, too."

As the song drifts away, the lead singer in the band welcomes everyone, introduces the members, and begins to play covers of new and old country music. We sit and listen for a few songs. When "Copperhead Road" begins to play, all the girls in the place head toward the dance floor. Raegan looks at me.

"I'll be right back." She stands and makes her way to the dance floor. Her hips sway to the beat of the music, and as she reaches the dance floor, she tosses her hands into the air and begins to clap on beat, and before I know it, every female in the joint is in unison in a line dance. The Electric Slide has nothin' on this.

When the song comes to an end, she smiles as she walks back to me. I stand to meet her.

"Rae, when did 'Copperhead Road' get its own line dance?" I question.

"Maybe a year ago or somethin'. I'm not real sure." As the band continues to turn out more country tunes, it doesn't take long for Raegan and me to find a spot on the dance floor. The playlist from the band is kick ass, and as they get ready to break, they slow it down. I take my arms, pull them a little tighter around Raegan, and we begin to move to the music like the world just stopped spinning.

"Hey, Em, you wanna Two-Step?" she inquires as she burns those deep emerald eyes into mine.

"Sure."

She takes my hand, and we jump in line with the crowd around us. It's been a while since I've done this, but it takes no time for me to fall right in time with Raegan. She smiles at me, and I know I'm done. It's taken me all of two days back in my hometown to fall for the girl who's been in my dreams for years.

As the song ends, I lead her away from the dance floor to the bar area to get a drink.

"Rae, whatcha want to drink?" I ask.

"Sun Drop would be fabulous!" she says.

We take our drinks and notice our table is gone, but that's not a problem. It just gives me a reason to stand closer to her. After we finish our drinks, we make our way back to the floor. Glancing over my shoulder, I see Cole making his way in with his friends. I toss my head back and give my full attention to Raegan.

Before long, Cole and his friends are making their rounds with the ladies on the dance floor. Raegan looks his way and smiles, and then he makes his way toward us.

"Hey, Rae!" Cole yells over the music.

"Hey! Catch anything?" she asks.

"A few bream and a catfish or two," he says as he begins to dance with his flavor of the night.

"I'll expect that for supper tomorrow!" He laughs and forgets I'm standing there. I hate for the thought to enter my head, but I feel like there is something about these two that I just don't know.

As if right on cue, Raegan places her hand upon my chest and grins at me. When she brings those gorgeous lips to mine, that thought evaporates from my mind. I swear, never in a million years did I expect to roll back into Pleasant Hill and feel like I never left. Raegan is my home, and knowing I wasted all that time with a cheating ex makes me wish I could relive this summer again. Then again, it's made me the person I am today, and I wouldn't trade the memories we've just begun to build for the world.

After talking to Cole a few more minutes I notice the time, and I know it's time to get her home. I sure don't want a shotgun waiting on me when I get back. I place my arm around her waist and whisper in her ear as we make our way out the door.

CHAPTER 10

Raegan

When Emmett whispers in my ear that it's time to go, goosebumps rise on my skin. I bite my lip and nod in agreement as we make our way outside. Our ride to the farm is filled with laughter and a desire to constantly touch each other. I hear Dustin Lynch begin to play through the radio, and before I know what's going on, Emmett has pulled the truck off the side of the highway with the engine running. I stifle a laugh as he runs to open my door and squeal as he takes my hand and pulls me to the ground and into his perfectly rock solid body. We sing to each other while moving to the beat as random cars continue down the two-lane highway past us.

On the final beat of the music, Emmett takes my cheek in his hand, my mind races as he pulls my lips to his, and he kisses me like his life depends on it. This has to be the best kiss of my life. If I thought I saw stars at the field party, I just got caught in an entire constellation. When I'm brought back to reality, I know that in this moment, this boy is going to change my life.

Emmett leads me to the truck and gets back in the

driver's side. He looks my way, and I melt right there on the spot. He puts the truck into drive, and we both can't erase the grins on our faces. Tonight is a night for the history books. Not only have I had an awesome date, but it's with someone that totally gets me. I can't wait to see where the two of us are headed.

As we pull into the driveway, I can't keep my lips off of his. He laughs and kisses me again before walking me to the door. Placing my hand on the doorknob, I look back at him and smile. I wave to him before opening the front door and closing it behind me. I press my back against it as it closes. *What has this boy done to me?* I must be grinning like an opossum because Grandaddy rounds the corner and cackles.

"What?" I ask as my cheeks flush pink.

"Nothin,' Sunshine. Nothin'," he says as he makes his way back into the kitchen. Shaking my head, I follow him. I go to the freezer and grab a tub of homemade snow cream from this winter and two spoons before sitting across from him. Opening the container, I wait for him to ask the first question. "So, whatcha do tonight?" he asks lightly.

Taking the spoon, I skim the top of the snow cream and place it into my mouth before answering, "He took me to eat at Smoke, and then we went to The Shed."

"And…" he says slowly as he takes his turn in the snow cream.

"And… we saw Cole there."

He looks up from the snow cream and stares at me like I caught him off guard. "What'd he have to say?"

"That we've got supper tomorrow."

"Allll righhht!" He finishes dipping his spoon into the snow cream. "So, Sunshine, tell me a little more about this date. He didn't try anything, did he?"

"Grandaddy!" I gasp. "I can't believe you!"

"What? I'm just makin' sure. I'd hate for this old man to have to show him who's boss." We both laugh.

"Actually, Grandaddy, he was a perfect gentleman...most of the time," I say with a giggle as I text Jordyn quickly about the kiss that just changed my life.

Jordyn: I want deets! Not just a text!

Me: K I'll call ya in morning, talkin to Gdaddy now

"It's times like these I wish your mawmaw or mama was here. I don't know if I can handle all of this, but I'll sure try," he says honestly.

"I know this much. Never in my seventeen years has a guy treated me like he does, except you. He acts like I'm the only girl in the room, but best of all, Grandaddy, he sees me for me, not the girl everyone expects me to be."

Grandaddy doesn't say anything else. He takes another couple of bites, and then finally replies, "Raegan, you deserve someone to love you completely, not because of your last name, what happened to our family, or what people think about you, but because of the bright and compassionate star you are. If anyone wants to think otherwise, then they don't deserve you." He takes another bite.

Water begins to creep into my eyes. "I love you, Grandaddy, and life tossed us a big curveball, but I wouldn't want it any other way."

Grandaddy tries to divert his eyes from mine, but I catch a glimpse of them shimmering. "Sunshine, dang right. I'm glad God saved me for you that night. We've been on this road a long time, and I know we don't know the future. I do, however, know I feel better knowing you have Emmett in yours."

I'm unable to control the waterworks as I shake my head in agreement. No matter what those doctors told him, or he says they told him, I have a feeling in the pit of my stomach that tells me something different.

Grandaddy stands. "Come here, Sunshine." I stand and walk toward him, and he holds me as we both cry. When there aren't any more tears to shed, he pulls back and looks at me. "No more tears, Sunshine. For both of us."

"Okay," I say as he gives me one more squeeze before we call it a night.

As I walk to my room, I remove my accessories and feel completely drained emotionally. I toss on my pajamas, wash my face, and brush my teeth before sliding into the bed. Grabbing my stuffed bunny, I hold it in my arms like I did when I was five years old and cry myself to sleep.

Emmett

As soon as I make it out to the main road, I crank up the radio and smile, because I know Raegan feels a connection between us too. Once I'm home, I grab a drink and a bag of chips before watching *SportsCenter* on ESPN and calling it a night. At some point, I wake up to the TV still on and chip crumbs on the couch. *Dang! Mom's gonna kill me.* I quickly clean up my mess and make my way to my room. Just as I'm about to meet Raegan in my dreams, the house phone rings, and everybody knows that a phone call this late at night can never be good.

I hurry to the hallway to see what's going on when Mom meets me halfway.

"Em, Cole's been in an accident. I don't know much. All I know is it's not real good right now. Throw on a shirt and let's go," she says with distress in her voice.

"Yes, ma'am." I hustle to my room, slide on the first shirt

and pair of shoes I can find and meet George and her in the car. *Rae. I've gotta call Rae!*

"George, can I call Rae? I think she and Mr. Lowery would wanna be there," I say with a little hesitation in my voice.

"Please," he says.

CHAPTER 11

Raegan

Waking up to the sound of my phone vibrating on the nightstand, I see Emmett's name, and I can't help but smile, even though I feel like I've been run over by a Mack truck.

"Hey," I mumble half-asleep, but attempting to sound like I'm awake.

"Rae! It's Cole! He's been in an accident," he races to say with terror in his voice. I realize it's not morning, and I pray I'm not reliving a nightmare that occurred twelve years ago.

"Em, we're on our way. Do we need to get you?"

"No, I'm with George and Mom," he says.

"I'm getting Grandaddy now." I press *End* on my phone, toss it onto my bed, and run to Grandaddy's room.

"Grandaddy! We've got to go to the hospital. It's Cole. He's been in an accident." Grandaddy sits up in a hurry when he hears the word "accident," and I know he's reliving more vividly what I barely remember.

"Get dressed and meet me in the kitchen in five."

Shutting the door, I run to my room, toss on my shorts from tonight, a bra, tank top, and pull on my boots. I don't bother with my hair, teeth, or anything. Instead, I grab a ball cap and hurry to meet Grandaddy. He walks in right after me. I toss him the keys, and we haul tail to get to Cole in time.

Emmett

Once we arrive at the hospital, George goes back to see Cole. Mom decides to give them a little privacy, and we take a seat in the waiting area.

"Mom, you can go with him if you want. I can wait on Mr. Lowery and Rae out here."

She shakes her head no. "George and Cole are a pair. They have been each other's rocks since his mom left all those years ago. They need time to themselves. George will assess the situation and come get us if he thinks it's that bad."

I start to comment, but then I see the doors open. Rae looks pale as a ghost and almost on the verge of breaking. When her eyes meet mine, I see into her soul. She's afraid of what might happen if she loses someone else. Running into my arms like I'm her saving grace, she begins to cry, and between sobs, she asks if he's gonna be okay.

Raegan

I swear, if I didn't know any better, I'd think my grandaddy was a NASCAR driver. He puts the truck in the wind, and we are at the local hospital in a matter of minutes. We find a parking spot and hustle to the front doors. As they slide open, I see Emmett and his mom standing there. I run to his arms.

"He's gonna be okay, right?" I ask as I sob in his arms.

"We don't know. It's a waiting game. His dad's back

there right now," he answers as I pull back and wipe the tears.

Grandaddy turns to Emma, Emmett's mom. "Can I go back there?"

"I'm sure, Dover. You're family," she says quietly.

"Sunshine, I'll be right back." He looks directly at Emmett. "Don't let her outta your sight."

"Yes, sir."

Grandaddy makes his way to the nurses' desk and into the back. Emmett pulls me close, and I take a seat with him and his mom. Never in my life did I expect to sit in the hospital waiting room, waiting to find out a family member's fate from another car accident.

We wait for what feels like an eternity before George and Grandaddy walk out. Cole's dad looks like like a ghost, and Grandaddy is putting on a show, but I can read his emotions like a book.

"How is he?" I ask. They don't' say anything; they just walk toward us. *Please, God, no!* "Grandaddy?!" I scream. He walks up to me, squeezes my hand, and looks me in the eye. *Oh my god! Please tell me he's not gone.* I feel my breathing increase, and I'm on the verge of hyperventilating.

"Sunshine, slow down. Take a deep breath," he says calmly. I try to do as he says, but fear consumes my body. I can't do this again. "He's gonna be a'ight. It's gonna take a while, but he will pull through." I crumble in Grandaddy's arms as tears of joy pour from my eyes. "Do you wanna go see him?"

"Yeah, but shouldn't Em and his mom go first?" I ask as I look around to his family. His dad informs us that Emmett and I should see Cole now, because they are going to be here all night and will see him when we come out.

I look at Grandaddy as Emmett waits for me. "It will be okay, Sunshine. I promise." Then, Emmett takes me by the hand, and we walk to face Cole in a hospital bed.

Once Emmett and I are alone in the hallway, he turns to look at me. "Are you okay?" I shake my head yes. "I don't believe you."

"I just never pictured coming back to this place for another accident. It's like someone's playing a sick joke on us," I say. He wraps his arm around my shoulder, pulls me close, kisses my forehead, and we make our way to Cole.

CHAPTER 12

Raegan

As we walk into Cole's room, I brace myself for what I might see. Trying to make it the worst-case scenario will at least lighten the actual results, even if they are bad.

When Emmett opens the door, I take a deep breath and see Cole lying in a hospital bed looking lifeless. There are cords attached everywhere, the room is dimly lit, and I stare at his chest to see if it is moving.

Walking toward the bed, I see his eyes are opening, and he's trying to look at us. I let go of Emmett and hurry to his side.

"Cole, it's me," I say as I grab his hand in mine. He starts to speak. "Shhh...Don't talk." He ignores me.

Softly, Cole says, "Rae, I'm so sorry. You shouldn't have to be here like this again."

"Stop, Cole. I'm just glad you're alright," I counter as I begin to cry again. Emmett walks closer and pulls me tighter while I continue to hold onto Cole's hand. We don't say anything else; we just silently pray he's going to be okay. After about twenty minutes of silence, Emmett says we probably should let the others come in. I shake my head and lean over

Cole, giving him a kiss on the cheek. "I love you, Cole." He tells me he loves me, too, and Emmett informs him he will return later.

Grandaddy, George, and Emma are waiting for us when we walk back into the waiting area. We don't say a lot, but his parents go back into the room after they insist that Emmett goes home.

As the three of us make our way out to the parking lot, we all slide into Grandaddy's truck. We drive toward Emmett's house, and after we drop him off, I'm taken back in time to when I made this journey with my grandaddy after the funerals, but instead of Johnny Cash, I hear Luke Bryan's "Drink A Beer," and I'm blessed that Cole is still with us. Grandaddy doesn't say a word; he pats my thigh, letting me know he understands and assuring me it's gonna be alright.

Once we get to the farm, we make our way inside and back to bed. It won't be long before the sun comes up. I set my alarm, because I know even though it's Sunday, there is still work to be done before church.

I wake up to the sound of my alarm, and my body feels as if it has just fallen back asleep. I take a deep breath before pushing the cover aside and doing what has to be done.

Emmett

Watching Raegan and Mr. Lowery leave in the truck is rough. I know I'm walking into an empty house and unsure of when things will return to normal. When I can no longer see the taillights, I close the door and make my way inside. I don't bother going to my room; I just sprawl out on the couch.

As I try to drift off to sleep, my mind wanders to Cole and how things are going to change in his life. Not being able to work is gonna be rough on him, but Raegan, I just don't know if I can handle seeing her hurt like I did today. It killed me to watch her in pain. When she hurts, I feel it in my soul. Finally, when my eyes can no longer stay open, sleep consume me.

CHAPTER 13

Emmett

As the sun begins to peer through the curtains into my eyes, I roll over on the couch, feeling like I've been sleeping on a piece of plywood and a transfer truck has run over my body. It's no use to try to get comfortable. I look at my phone to see if I've missed anything, but nothing's there.

Sitting up, I take a moment to rub my eyes, and call Mom to see how Cole is doing.

"Hey, Mom. How's he doin' this mornin'?" I question.

"Better. They hope he's gonna be able to go home in a few days, even though he won't be able to go to work for at least a week or more. I don't know how we're gonna keep him from the farm," she says with a hint of laughter in her voice, and that's how I know it will all be okay. After telling her I'll be by in a little while, we hang up. I toss my phone onto the table and lie back down, closing my eyes for just a few more minutes.

Somehow I drift back to sleep, but wake up to the buzzing of my phone. Still half-asleep, I fumble around the table, trying to grab it. *Got it!* I look down to see Raegan's name, and I'm suddenly awake and feeling like a million bucks.

Raegan

Grandaddy and I feed the animals and gather the eggs and once we're finished we clean-up for breakfast.

"Rae, are you up to church this mornin'?" he asks between sips of coffee.

"Yeah, but after church, I think I might need a nap," I say.

"I'm right there with ya. We can go visit Cole on our way home from church. Maybe we should take George and Emma lunch. I think I'll call and see if that works for them."

"Okay." We finish breakfast, and I clean the kitchen before getting ready for church. I want to call Emmett, but I'm afraid he might be sleeping. I'd hate to wake him if he was, so I decide to shower and get ready first and then call him.

As the scalding water runs over my body, I feel a wave of relief and refreshment. I could stay in this spot forever, but eventually, I'd turn into a prune. Then, the relief is replaced with memories of last night. I try to push them to the side, but I can't. Closing my eyes, I see Cole lying in the hospital bed, and when I open them, I can still hear Emmett's voice in my head. Tears begin to stream down my face as I try to escape my current situation. Yet again, someone I love is hurt due to an accident. I just pray this is where it ends. I don't know if I can be strong much longer, especially if something happens to Grandaddy. As a sob expels from my lungs, I reach deep within my soul. I have to be strong. They both need me. I take a deep breath and hold it as the water pours down my face. As I exhale the air from my lungs, I turn off the water, grab a towel, and dry off quickly before getting ready for church. Once I'm finished, I pick up my phone and text Emmett.

Me: Em, just wanted to let you know you were

on my mind. Call me when you wake up.

Within minutes, my phone rings, and I hear the raspy, yet tender voice of Emmett on the other side.

"Mornin', Rae. Are you okay?" he asks.

"I'm okay, but the question is, how are you?" I hope he can't sense what I have been feeling all morning.

He doesn't say anything for a moment. "I feel like I've been run over, but hearing your voice makes everything better." I smile at the thought of my voice making him better.

"I understand that completely. I'm goin' with Grandaddy to church and to see Cole after. Have you heard anything this mornin'?" I question.

"Yeah, Mom called and said he is comfortable and making some improvements. They said they hoped he would go home in a day or two if his improvements continue. I'm goin' by there in just a few."

"I'll see you there in a little while then. We're bringin' lunch, too."

"Y'all don't have to do that," he says.

"Yeah, we do. Y'all need to eat, and I'm sure you can only eat so much hospital food." We both laugh, and that feels good.

Relieved that Cole is going to be okay, Emmett and I talk for a few minutes. I enjoy living in the present and not thinking about last night. Cole was lucky; I *was* lucky because he's the only one that knows the secret, and I can't make it through this without him.

CHAPTER 14

Raegan

Grandaddy and I enjoy church and are asked a gazillion questions about Cole. Of course, everyone thinks alcohol was involved, but it wasn't. Cole's smarter than that. I swear, some people are just idiots.

Once church is over, we pull through KFC for a family meal and make our way toward the hospital. I sneak a potato wedge from the bag.

"I saw that, Sunshine," Grandaddy says. "Now, pass one this way." I smile and hand him one. *I love him more than life itself.*

Once we arrive at the hospital, we carry the food inside and head to Cole's room. He's now been moved to a room that will allow more than two visitors at a time, and he's sitting up when we enter.

"Cole!" I exclaim as I drop the food onto the counter by the sink and rush to hug him.

"Rae, I'm okay, girl. No need to freak out," he says lightly.

"If you weren't lying in a hospital bed, I'd hit you right

now!" I say as I put my hands on my hips. He starts to laugh until it hurts too much.

I hear Emmett laughing in the background. My eyes meet his, and I walk to him. His arms open, and I fall right into them. *I sure hope Grandaddy doesn't kill him!* He gives me a light kiss on the top of my head, and it reminds me of Saturday night. My cheeks start to creep red, but I try to hide it because I don't want any questions.

When we pull apart, I walk back to the food. "Y'all ready to eat?" I ask.

"Thank you so much, Dover and Raegan. Y'all didn't have to do this," Emma says.

"Yes, we did," Grandaddy answers.

Once we eat, Emma and George go home while we visit. When Cole becomes too tired, we tell him we'll see him later, and the three of us make our way outside.

"Sunshine, why don't you ride with Emmett? This old man can handle it by himself for a while," Grandaddy says as we reach his truck.

I look at Emmett, and he smiles. "Are you sure?" I question.

"I'm sure. Go have some fun."

"Okay," I say as I hug him goodbye, and then I lace my hand in Emmett's, and we make our way to his truck. He opens the door for me, and we drive out of the parking lot. "So, what are we gonna do?" I ask him. He looks at me and gives me that panty droppin' smile. *Oh, lawd!*

"Whatcha wanna do?" he banters back.

"Doesn't matter to me, but I wanna get outta this dress!" I say without thinking about the words that just left my mouth. Emmett's mouth drops, and I can see that he's a total guy. It makes me laugh. "Get that mind outta the gutter! Would you wanna stay in something like this all day?" He shakes his head no.

"How 'bout I take you to change, and then we can do whatever you wanna do?"

"Works for me," I say, and Emmett takes me to the farm. Grandaddy is shocked when we pull up behind him, but it takes him no time to realize why we are here. Once I change, I tell him goodbye again and hurry back to Emmett in the truck.

Emmett

When Raegan comes jogging out of the house in a pair of Daisy Dukes and a tank top with her hair pulled back through a ball cap, I about lose it. Not to mention, how I almost lost it ten minutes ago, when she told me she wanted to get out of her dress. This girl is making me go crazy, but heck, it's a good kinda crazy.

As she makes her way to my truck, I lean over and open the door for her. She smiles and hops inside.

"What do we do now?" she questions with a cute little grin.

"What's there to do fun 'round here?"

"Well, we could go fishin', hang out by the creek, or just cruise out in the country. That's 'bout it."

"Let's ride around, and you show me what I've missed since I've been gone."

"A'ight," she says. "Can you stop at the store, so I can grab a Sun Drop real quick?"

"Sure." I say as we make our way back to the main road.

Once we're at the store, I fill up with gas, and she goes in to get a drink and snack. "Rae! Don't you pay for that!" I yell as she walks inside, acting like she doesn't hear me. *Um, I could watch that backside move all day.* I leave the gas pumping as I hurry inside before she pays. Of course, she's already grabbed me a drink as well. "Thank ya. Will you check on the gas? I got this," I tell her. She wants to argue, but instead, she gives me a quick kiss on the cheek.

I walk to the counter and pay for our food and wait until the gas is finished. The clerk looks at me and shakes her head. I must look at her with a confused look.

"Honey, you've got it bad, don't ya?" I just smile, but don't answer. "It's okay. It happens to the best of ya. She's a good one, and her grandaddy is as good as gold."

"Yes, he is," I agree before taking the bag and exiting the store.

Raegan is already waiting in the passenger seat with her feet propped up on the dash and her arm hanging out of the window. *Each time I think she can't look any hotter, she does.* "Here ya go," I say as I hand her drink and candy bar to her.

"Thanks, Em, but you didn't have to get it," she says.

"Yes, I did. You're with me, and as long as that's the case, you won't buy anything." Shock covers her face, but it is soon replaced with a smile. She sits up in her seat, unbuckles, and moves toward the console to meet me in the driver's seat. When her lips touch mine, my hand rises to meet her neck. Forgetting where we are, we pull back and laugh when the driver behind us honks his horn. I pull her in for one more quick kiss, and then she moves back to her seat. This girl's got me hook, line, and sinker. I swear, I'm glad she picked me out of that pond, 'cause every moment I spend with her feels like I just won the Bassmasters.

As we cruise around town, Raegan points out *everything* that has changed since I left, and when she's not talking, she's singing to the music on the radio. When there's nothing else to tell, she looks at me.

"I've got an idea!" she says excitedly.

"You're makin' me nervous," I joke with her.

"Let's head to the creek."

I make a right, and we head to the creek at the edge of the Lowery's farm. We pull down the side of the road before I find a place to park.

Putting the truck into park, I look at her. "Now what?" I ask.

"Mr. Bridges, I think it's time to do a little creek stompin'!" she says as she jumps outta my truck and runs to the creek. I shake my head and hurry to catch up with her.

Just as she's about to reach the water, I grab her and pull her up into my arms. She wraps her arms around my neck and smiles at me. "Em, there's nowhere I'd rather be than here with you." She kisses me gently as I place her back onto the ground. "Come on," she says as she pulls me by the hand and runs into the water, shoes and all.

We spend the next hour wandering up the creek, moving from rock to rock, stomping in the water, and trying to catch fish with our bare hands. I have to say; this is the best idea I've ever heard from a girl.

By the time we make it back to where we started, we are soaking wet, and she is by far the most beautiful person I've ever met— inside and out. As she's about to head out of the creek, I call her name, and when she turns around, I hit her with a big wave of water.

"Oh, no, you didn't!" she hollers, and it's on. She begins tossing water my way, and I do the same.

"Stop, Em!" she squeals as I hit her with more water. I laugh and just continue splashing her. When I know she's about to get pissed, I stop.

As soon as I let down my guard, she hits me with a wave of water that leaves me speechless. "You've done it now!" I say and make my way to her. She tries to hurry out of the water, but I catch her, pick her up, and place her back into the water. This time I fall in with her. We both giggle and then stop when we gaze into each other's eyes. As I bring my lips to hers, I get soaked with water, yet again, and she jumps up, laughing and running toward the truck.

The moment Raegan is out of the water, I can't do anything but stare, mouth wide open, gonna catch a mouth full of flies, gawking. Yup, that's what she does to me, but when she starts to flat out belly laugh near the truck, I can't take it anymore. I have to be near her, to touch her, and to let her know it's okay to be this way with me.

The closer I get to her, the more she tries to stop laughing, and the more I want to help her stop. She begins to step backward until she is flush with the side of my truck. When she begins to apologize to me, I want to tell her there's no reason to apologize, but when my name rolls off her tongue, I just have to let it.

Taking one final step to make sure there is minimal space between us, I place my hands on each side of her face and look into her eyes.

"Rae, that wasn't funny."

"I'm sorry. I just can't quit laughin'. I swear, I've not laughed like this in forever.

"Rae, there's no reason to apologize to me, but if you want me to be honest, I will." She looks as me with an unsure expression, but nods yes. "Hearing you laugh is like music to my ears, but hearing you say my name makes me want to shout from the rooftop that you're mine. Raegan, will you be mine?" Rather than responding, she grabs my shirt and attacks my lips.

CHAPTER 15

Raegan

As Emmett's body traps mine against the truck he lays it all out onto the table. Unsure of what to say, I just react. I grab his still dripping, wet shirt in my hand and bring his lips to meet mine.

"So, Rae, you didn't answer my question," he says between kisses.

"Yes, Em, I'll be yours," I reply and then press my lips to his again.

"You're not ready to go yet, are you?" he asks with his forehead against mine. I shake my head no. In fact, I don't know how I'm ever gonna leave his sight again.

"Come here," he says as he walks to the back and lowers the tailgate. He lifts me up and sits me there while placing himself between my legs. I circle my arms around him and rest my forehead against his. "Hold on a sec," he commands as he steps away and goes around to the driver's side. He turns on the ignition and the radio, grabs our drinks, and comes back to sit beside me. "Here ya go."

"Thanks," I say as my feet dangle below, and I wish he were wedged between my legs again.

We sit and listen to the music and enjoy the southern sunshine. I think about this morning and how my day has turned out differently than I had planned, but it's a million times better than I could have imagined.

"Rae, can I ask you somethin'?" he questions.

"Sure."

"What are y'all gonna do with Cole outta work for a while?"

"I guess we just do what we've been doin'. Why do you ask?" *I know why he's asking. It's sweet, but I can't let him be that close to me, not with Grandaddy's situation being unknown.*

"I thought I could help if you needed an extra hand," he suggests.

"Thanks, but let us just try it alone for a while. If it changes, I'll let you know. Hopefully, Cole won't be gone too long," I say.

Emmett grabs my chin and turns me to face him. "Rae, it's okay to ask for help. I'd be glad to do it, but I understand how things are with y'all. Just know if you change your mind, I'd be glad to."

"Okay," I say as we sit and listen to the birds chirp and the water ripple down the creek.

When the sun begins to set, I know it's time to get back, and Emmett realizes it, too. He pushes off the tailgate and comes to face me again. He places his body exactly where I wish it had remained. "Thank you for a wonderful day." Then, he lays his hand on the bill of my ball cap and removes it. Setting it to the side, he runs his hand in my hair before letting it come to a rest on my cheek. He looks as if he's trying to find the words, but he doesn't say anything. Instead, he kisses me on that tailgate, and for once, I'm glad it's not a tipsy tailgate kissing kinda night.

Emmett

I don't want to see what time it is, but I don't have a choice, and I realize we need to get back. We are both exhausted, and we have school tomorrow. I scoot off the tailgate and place my body between her legs, yet again. Before I let my mind wander to inappropriate thoughts of us, I thank her, and then I do what I've been dying to do since she walked out of that house. I remove her ball cap and run my fingers through her brown locks until I stop on her cheek. I want to tell her how much I've thought about her over the years, but I don't. *What guy does that?* Instead, I remain silent and kiss her long and hard on the back of my tailgate.

"Em, we better get goin'," she declares as we pull apart, and as much as I hate to admit it, she's right.

The ride back to the farm doesn't take long, so I drive extra slow since we are already on their property. When we make it back to her driveway, panic begins to set in. We are both soaking wet and look like we've been doing who knows what.

She glances my direction. "Are you okay?" she asks as she moves her hand to mine.

"Yeah, I'm just kinda worried what your grandaddy is gonna think about us." She has a confused look on her face. "Rae, we're soakin' wet, and I have no idea what he's gonna think we've been doin'."

"There's no need to worry. I tell him everything anyway." She smirks.

"Everything?"

"Yup, we have no secrets between us." Taking a big gulp, I'm suddenly glad I didn't let things go further.

CHAPTER 16

Raegan

The look on Emmett's face when I tell him there are no secrets between Grandaddy and me is priceless. It is the truth, though. There aren't any secrets; well, except maybe one that he's asked me to keep. I push that to the side and rub my thumb against his.

"Em, no worries. He likes you... a lot, actually." *I can't believe Grandaddy's all about this guy.* "That's a relief." Emmett reaches over and guides his hand behind my neck before pulling my lips to his. "I guess I'll see ya in the mornin'," he says.

Mornin'. This is going to be interesting. "Em, I can't see ya soon enough." He smiles at me as I make my way to the front door. It's better he doesn't walk me to the door, since our clothing situation isn't the same as how we left.

"Grandaddy!" I holler as I walk inside. "I'm home!" I glance in the kitchen and living room, but I don't see him anywhere. I start to freak out as I make my way from room to room. *Where is he?* Walking back to the front of the house, I notice his truck parked in its usual spot. *Maybe he went back to see Cole.* I take out my phone and start to call him when I see a note on the kitchen table. *Go figure!*

Sunshine,
Rode with Joe to visit Cole again. I should be back by 8. There's a pizza in the freezer if you want to eat it for supper. Love you to the moon and back!
G-daddy

I smile, thinking pizza sounds fabulous. Grabbing my phone, I call Jordyn. I can't wait to tell her about what happened today and the fact that I'm officially Emmett Bridge's girl.

After Jordyn finishes squealing, she tells me how excited she is and how we *have* to go on a double date with Ridge and her, then we talk about what's going on this week before I let her go.

Once we hang up, I place the pizza in the oven, I hurry upstairs to shower and change while it bakes. I smile as the warm water covers my body. To think that earlier today, I fell apart in here, but right now, I couldn't feel more alive.

I hurry to get back downstairs before the pizza looks more like burnt toast. As I take a seat in the living room and turn on the TV, I see headlights coming up the driveway. *Grandaddy.*

"Sunshine, I'm home," he says as I hear his keys hit the table. He comes into the living room. "Did y'all have fun?" he questions.

"We did," I answer with my mouth half full of food. After I finish that bite, I give him a rundown of my afternoon with Emmett. When I get to the creek stompin' part, he smiles and laughs just like I did. My heart warms knowing he's happy for me.

"Sunshine, Emmet's a good guy, but remember, he's a guy."

"Grandaddy!"

"Hey, I'm just callin' it like I see it, but if I had to choose someone for you, I'd choose him."

"What makes you say that?" I ask.

He takes a seat beside me. "That boy sees the real you. He gets that you're just Raegan, not the girl who lost her parents or the girl that has everything going for her. I saw how he looked when you walked into that hospital room today, and Sunshine, he's got it bad."

I start to giggle. Grandaddy has never liked to talk about boys or the birds and the bees with me. His tone turns serious.

"Sunshine, we don't know what our future holds, but I know I want a man that loves you for you, and Emmett Bridges is it for you."

My grandaddy's words go straight to the heart, and I know he's telling the truth. Even with the way Emmett looks at me and the way I feel about him, there's only one person that would ever cause me to venture away from him—the most important man in my life that is sitting right next to me.

Emmett

As Raegan makes her way inside, I can't help but repeat those words over and over. *No secrets. No secrets between them.* Oh, I'm dead. Dover Lowery is going to hunt me down and shoot me if we take things any further. I shake my head to try to clear my mind, crank up the radio, and drive home.

I call Mom on my way to see if they are still at the hospital, and they are on their way home as well. I stop and grab a bite to eat, and once I'm home, I notice that Jace is in the front yard shooting some hoops. *Here we go.*

"What's up, Jace?" I ask as his hard stare meets me, and I realize he's probably wondering where I've been.

"Not much." As soon as I put the key into the lock, it starts. "Quick question," he says, and I turn to face him.

"Shoot," I say.

"How is it that you walk back into town and the girl that is untouchable falls at your feet?"

"Dude, really?" I say sarcastically as he puts down the ball and walks toward me.

"Just curious, because it makes sense for Raegan and me to be together, but you show up, and I'm history," he says with his arms crossed.

"Look, all I know is it just kinda happened. It's not like we're strangers. I'm not a new kid on the block. I'm an old kid that's back on the block." I turn to go inside.

"Well, just know that one day she's gonna have to choose between you and her grandaddy, and that's not a choice for her. Remember that," he says with irritation in his voice as he goes back to shooting hoops.

"Yeah, I gotcha man." I don't have time for stupid assholes like him. *Dumb ass,* I think to myself as I walk inside and up to my room to get out of these wet clothes. As I remove them, I can't help but think how I'd love to remove Raegan's right off her body.

CHAPTER 17

Raegan

Monday's alarm clock comes way before the crack of dawn. I slept like a baby last night and jump out of bed, because I know the sooner I get moving, the sooner I'm done with my chores and off to school. It's five o'clock. That means three hours until I get to see Emmett. A smile spreads across my face, and I throw on work clothes and make my way downstairs.

The kitchen light is already on as well as the light inside the barn. *Man, why didn't I beat him this morning? He needs to take it easy.* I grab my boots and sit on the porch to slide them on before I head to the barn.

"Mornin', Sunshine," Grandaddy says as he feeds each of the horses in their stalls.

"Mornin'. Whatcha need me to start with?" I ask.

"I'll feed them if you'll check the water, collect the eggs, and slop the hogs. I should be able to handle the rest today."

Standing there with my hands on my hips, I reply, "Grandaddy, you better not work too hard today!"

"Now, listen. Before you get all feisty like your mawmaw, hold up. Joe's coming back mid-mornin'. We have this covered. I don't want you to worry. You got me?" he says firmly.

"Yes, sir. I'm glad Joe's comin'," I say, and it's the truth. Joe is my grandaddy's longest childhood friend and a lawyer in town. They might be getting up there in age, but those men know how to work. They'd put guys my age to shame. "I'll hurry, so I can get breakfast ready, too."

Within the hour, I'm finished and making my way back inside the house. I take a package of fresh bacon and a few fresh eggs from the fridge. Once breakfast is complete, I go out to tell Grandaddy. As we eat together, we talk about the day and plans for the week. After breakfast, I get ready for school while he goes back out to start working for the day.

Hustling to get ready, I shower and let my damp hair dry naturally. I look in my closet and have no idea what to wear. Not that it really matters, because I know Emmett doesn't care, but images are important when you are *the Raegan Lowery.* I choose a pair of neon pink shorts, an embellished black tank, and a pair of gladiator sandals. After I finish putting on my makeup and scrunching my hair with a little gel, I grab my backpack and make my way downstairs to tell Grandaddy goodbye before leaving.

I see him at the tractor shed. I toss my bag into my truck before I walk his way. When he notices me, he stops what he's doing and walks toward me.

"A'ight, Grandaddy, I'm gone. I'll see ya this afternoon. You and Joe behave, okay?" I tell him as I hug him.

"Sunshine, I don't know if Joe and I know how to stay outta trouble, but if not, we know a good lawyer."

"Oh my! That's enough." I laugh. "I'll see ya right after practice. Love you."

"Love you, too, and don't you worry 'bout this old man

or the farm. Do you hear me?"

"I hear ya," I say, heading to the truck.

I wave to him when I drive past him and make my way to school. I can't wait to lay my eyes on Emmett.

Emmett

When the alarm goes off, I hit *Snooze* at least five times. When I cut it off the last time, I pull myself from the bed. Sitting on the edge with my elbows on my knees, I give myself a minute to wake up. When Raegan's image enters my mind, I automatically become motivated.

Glancing at the clock, I hustle to get to school. I'm not exactly sure how this is gonna go now that Jace has said his peace, but I know I'm not gonna let him mess with her today.

Grabbing a quick shower, I shave to remove the stubble and then pull on a pair of AE khaki cargo shorts and a fitted vintage style tee. I grab a Pop Tart on the way out the door and put the truck in the wind.

When I arrive in the parking lot, I look for her truck, but I don't see it. *Crap! I didn't even find out how Cole was this morning!* I send Mom a quick text, and she says Cole's doing better, and they are going to work today because he insisted.

As I slide my phone back into my pocket, I see her blue Z71 Chevy coming in on two wheels. I can't help but smile, but when I see her hair blowing in the wind and the look on her face, laughter is the last thing from my mind. She's the hottest thing I've ever seen.

Raegan

Crap! Crap! Triple Crap! I'm running late! I push the

Chevy's gas pedal to the floorboard as I hurry to make it to school. This isn't how I planned on Monday starting. When I round the turn into the parking lot, my wheels squeal just a little as I slow down toward my parking space. Once I'm in my spot, I throw the truck into park, glance at my reflection in the rearview mirror, add a little lip-gloss, and grab my bag. As I turn from the truck, I see *him*. Who thought a pair of shorts and a tee could look so good? A smile escapes my lips, and I take a deep breath to slow myself down from my crazy drive to school this morning.

"Mornin,' Rae, or should I just call you Mario Andretti?" he teases as he approaches.

"I'll take that as a compliment," I say as I make my way to him. He embraces me in his arms, kisses the top of my head, and laces my fingers in his as we walk into Cleveland High. Emmett walks me to my locker as the first bell rings. "You better go, Em. I don't want you to be late because of me."

"It's all good. It'd just be my first tardy." *I guess he has a point.*

He walks me to physics and lets my hand go as I enter the doorway. I swear, every time he leaves me, I feel like a piece of me leaves, too. I take my seat and count the minutes until lunch.

When the bell rings, I gather my things and walk to my locker. I'm surprised when Jace smiles my way, but doesn't say a word. *Something is totally up with him.* I smile back and make my way to my next class, but not before someone wraps their arms around my waist as I walk.

"How was class?" Emmett asks.

"It was physics. Please, don't tell me you're takin' another tardy?" I laugh.

"Nah, I have physics next and just wanted to surprise

you."

"Thanks." I kiss him briefly on the cheek before he separates from me, and yet again, I'm yearning to have him near me.

Jordyn is waiting for me after class, and I know she's about to ask a gazillion and one questions, and to be honest, I can't wait to tell her all about it.

"Spill it, girlfriend!" Jordyn says with excitement. "But, first off, what happened to Cole? There are all these crazy rumors going on."

"Cole was in a car accident Saturday night. He hadn't been drinkin' or anything. Some car pulled out in front of him, and he tried to miss them, which he did, but not before he hit a freakin' tree. It was awful, J. I've never seen him so pitiful. That boy is like my brother, and I was scared I was gonna lose him."

"Can I be honest, Rae?" she asks.

"Aren't you always?" I laugh.

"True! I always thought he was in love with you."

"What? He's family for cryin' out loud." I've never in a million years looked at Cole that way. Now, I'll be the first to admit, he's easy on the eyes, but we are family.

"The way he looks at you sometimes, I mean, y'all are like barely related."

"Just stop! That's totally gross, and no, he's not in love with me. I know that for sure. Yuck! I don't even wanna think about that."

"Fine, I'll stop, because I'm tellin' ya right now, if I knew I stood any chance with him, I'd be all about that."

"We need a different subject because this is wrong on soooo many levels."

"Okay, so, what's up with you and Emmett? I overheard Jace talking this morning."

"What'd he say?" I stop in the hallway.

"He said he and Emmett had words last night. He made it sound like he was all big and bad, but my guess is he's the one that went inside with his tail between his legs." We both laugh because that is highly likely.

"Now, back to you. What's up with you and Emmett?" My face starts to flush red. "Ohmygosh! You're totally blushin', Rae! Spill it!"

"J, we had the best day. Well, after we left the hospital, anyway. Take out Cole's accident, and this has been the best weekend of my life. Emmett took me dancin' at The Shed Saturday, and then Grandaddy let me go with him yesterday after we left the hospital. We cruised around and then went to the creek."

"Y'all totally went creek stompin', didn't ya?"

"You know it!"

"I'd loved to have seen him all drippin' wet," Jordyn says seductively, and I laugh.

"It was nice."

"'Nice'? That's the word you're gonna use?" she asks. "'Nice' is how you tell Grandaddy he looks. I'm sure Emmett was like scrumptious!"

"Come to think of it, I think you're right," I say as I loop my arm in hers as we giggle our way toward the cafeteria.

Emmett

I'd planned on waiting for Raegan to walk into the cafeteria, but when I see her and Jordyn in a full-blown conversation, I decide to give them a little time.

Without much of an appetite, I settle on a pack of chips and a Gatorade from the vending machine and make my way to sit down. *Um, awkward! Do I sit with Jace like Friday or find a new table?* I see Ridge sitting at the table, and he makes a motion for me to move his way.

"What's up, Ridge? Jace?" I acknowledge them as I sit.

"We don't know. How 'bout you fill us in?" Ridge says with a sly grin.

"Besides spending the weekend in the hospital with Cole and Raegan showing me around town, that's been about it," I say, trying to keep it low key.

"I bet she showed you 'round town," Ridge says mockingly.

"Hey, man," I say as Ridge bursts out laughing.

"Chill. I'm just messin' with ya. We know Raegan is like the crown jewel, and nothing's getting that. Right, Jace?" He laughs.

Jace remains silent; he picks up his tray and walks outside. I laugh it off with Ridge until my eyes catch sight of Raegan and those long, toned legs moving our way.

"Who pissed in his Corn Flakes this mornin'?" Jordyn asks as she and Raegan sit at the table. *Did she really say that out loud?*

Ridge kisses her on the cheek. "Ya know, his macho ego just got deflated."

I smirk, and Raegan elbows me. "Play nice," she whispers.

"I didn't say a word." I throw up my hands to prove my innocence.

"Maybe not here, but word is there was a not-so-friendly discussion last night."

I just shrug my shoulders. I don't care to air out our business for everyone to hear.

"Em? What happened?" she asks as she places her hand

upon my leg. "I know he tries to act big and bad, but we all know he'd go cryin' to his mama. Tell me what happened."

"Nothin' really. He just wanted to know what was going on with us. So, I told him, left him standin' there, and went in and ate supper. That's pretty much it," I recount as I take a swig of my drink. Her eyes meet mine, and I can tell she's unsure if she believes me.

"I promise, Rae. That was it. I'm not arguing with him about you because there's no reason. You got me?"

"I got ya," she says as she lays her head upon my shoulder and steals my bag of chips.

"Chip thief? I never would have thought that about ya!" I tease as I watch her eat every last one as slow as possible.

CHAPTER 18

Raegan

The way Emmett stares at me as I eat his chips looks as if I am about to have him begging me to stop in front of everyone. I have to say, for a girl who hasn't really liked all the male attention I've gotten in the past, I love everything about the way Emmett Bridges looks, touches, and speaks to me.

When I finish the last chip, I don't give him time to think. Instead, I brush my salty lips across his and back away.

"Rae, you're gonna have to stop that," he says.

"What can I say? I love chips. Come on. We're gonna be late for class," I say as I stand from the table, grab his hand and we walk down the hallway.

The remainder of the day is filled with boring lectures, a pop quiz, and thoughts of Emmett. I take a few minutes with him after school before I head to practice. As I hurry to the gym from the locker room, Jace meets me.

"Hey, Raegan, you got a minute?" he asks as he stands propped against the wall.

"I've got like five. So, let's walk and talk 'cause I know you've got practice, too." *Can't he just get over it?* "Talk."

He takes a minute to look around, almost as if he's looking to see if anyone is watching. "Look, I don't know what he's got, but if he makes you happy, then I'm happy for you."

I stop mid-stride. "OMG! Is Jace admitting he is wrong?" I say smartly.

"Not funny. I'm trying to be nice here," he says.

"Sorry. Go on."

"I just wanted you to know I'm calling a truce. Not to say I like it, but I do want you to be happy. Of all the girls in this school, you deserve it."

I've never seen this side of Jace, and honestly, I don't believe it's genuine. "Thanks, that means a lot," I say as I give him a hug. He vanishes as quickly as he showed up. *Maybe I was wrong about him. Maybe he's not a total jackass, but regardless, he's not the guy for me.*

Practice goes off without a hitch, and I'm on my way home before I know it. When I get home, Grandaddy and Joe are sitting on the front porch sipping sweet tea and shooting the breeze.

"Hey, Sunshine," Grandaddy says as I meet him with a hug.

"Looks like y'all did all right today," I say to both of them.

"For two old buzzards, we still got it," Joe says, and we all laugh.

"I'm gonna fix us some supper. Have you heard any more about Cole today?" I ask Grandaddy.

"If things go well, he'll be home Wednesday. He's already tryin' to figure out how to get back to work. Bless him. He's gotta learn to take it easy."

"And you're one to talk," I say as I enter the house and start supper.

Emmett

I fall in love the minute Raegan steals my bag of chips. Most girls wouldn't be that bold as to steal their man's food within the first week of seeing each other, but when she eats each one slowly, I am fully aware that she knows exactly what she is doing to me.

When my mouth falls to the floor, she helps pick it up by placing her, salty with a hint of strawberry lip-gloss, lips onto mine. I try to keep her lips on mine a moment longer, but she pulls away and puts me back in our reality inside the school cafeteria, and I'm close to tardy number three today.

After school, I start to make my way to my truck, but decide to surprise her before practice. I'm caught off guard when I see her and Jace embracing in the gym. *I can't stand him! Why can't he get it through that dumb skull of his?* I shake it off and drive to the hospital. I mention to Cole what I saw, and he tells me not to worry, because he knows exactly how Raegan feels about Jace. That is much easier said than done.

After I get home, I take a quick run before supper and then see what Raegan's up to.

Me: Hope practice went okay. I can't wait to see you 2morrow.
Raegan: It did! Fixin' supper now and then I have a ton of homework. I can't wait to see you either.
Me: Try 2 come in on 4 wheels 2morrow. LOL
Raegan: HAHA I'll try! ;)

Tomorrow morning can't get here fast enough.

CHAPTER 19

Raegan

The next two days are near perfect. When I'm not working on the farm, I'm at school or practice. Every moment I can spend with Emmett, I do. Cole got discharged from the hospital on Wednesday morning, and as soon as practice is over, I make my way to visit.

As I pull into the driveway, I see Emmett's truck and smile. *This is kinda weird. I never thought the guy I'm head over heels for would live in this house.* Walking up to the door, I see Jace pulling in the driveway. *Dang.* I toss up my hand and wave before I ring the doorbell and wait for someone to answer. When the door opens, it's Emmett.

"Come in," he says as he takes my hand in his. "He's in his room."

"Okay." I say as I give him a brief kiss on the lips.

"Just give him a knock and go in. I'll give y'all some time."

A questioning look flashes in his eyes. *What's up with this giving us a minute? Whatever.* I shake it off. I give Cole's room a light knock and peek inside.

"Hey there, Rae," he says as he starts to sit up in the bed.

"Hey, how are ya feelin'?" I ask.

"I'm all right. Better than a few days ago. The question is, how are *you*?" I know exactly what he's referring to.

"I don't wanna talk about it," I say as I feel tears creeping up. I've fought them away all week, and I know the bewitching hour is upon us.

"Look, I know you don't, but just remember I'm here."

"I know."

"Has Uncle Dover said any more about it?" I shake my head no.

"Cole, I've got a really bad feelin' 'bout it. You know, the kind deep down in your gut that's never wrong."

He pats the bed beside him, and I take a seat. He moves my hair behind my ear. "Rae, it's gonna be okay. If he said the doctors aren't worried, then we shouldn't be either."

"I know, but..." is all I can manage before the waterworks flow.

"Listen to me, Rae. Don't do this. We don't know what's gonna happen tomorrow, but you're the strongest person I know. Have you said anything to Emmett?"

"No! Grandaddy said not to. I won't break that promise to him." He understands where I stand on that thought and drops it. He changes the subject, and I dry my eyes just in time for the blotchiness to evaporate from my face, as Grandaddy knocks on the door with Emmett right behind him.

"Hey, y'all," I say as they make their way into the room. We all visit, and then Emmett and I give Grandaddy and Cole some time alone. I can only imagine what is being said between those walls.

Emmett walks outside with me toward my truck. As I stand there with my back against the driver's side, he moves in closer and brings his lips to mine.

Emmett

As Raegan disappears behind Cole's door, I make my way back downstairs, but not before I hear her begin to cry. I know they are close, but he's getting better. What in this world would have her so upset? I begin to think about us, seeing her with Jace today, Jace's reaction at lunch, and their relationship. Feeling the frustration beginning to build, I walk out to my truck and clean out the Pop Tart wrappers from the week.

"Hey there, Emmett. How are you doin'?" I hear as I glance over my shoulder to see Mr. Lowery.

"I'm doing well, sir. How 'bout yourself?" I ask.

"A'ight, just thought I'd check on Cole. Where's Sunshine?"

"She's with Cole. I'm givin' them some time."

He crosses his arms and stands there. "Boy, let me tell ya somethin'. Don't ever get jealous of those two. Cole has been there for her as long as I can remember. They hit it off the day he started working in the summers when he was barely old enough to pick up a bale of hay, but not like you're thinking. Raegan has always been the girl everyone wants her to be, and you are the first guy to walk into her life that she's let in. Don't be a fool and screw it up because of what you think."

I'm completely floored by his forwardness. "Yes, sir. It's just hard to think through. Can I ask you one thing?"

"Go 'head."

"Well, you know my neighbor. Has she ever given him a thought?"

Mr. Lowery belly laughs in my face. "Son, Jace McCoy wants anything he can't have, and my Sunshine has wanted nothin', and I mean nothin', to do with him. You have no worries."

"Thanks for your honesty," I say to him.

"Anytime," he responds as he goes inside to talk to George and my mom.

When I finish, I walk back inside, and Mr. Lowery and I make our way to Cole's room. As we enter, Raegan is sitting beside Cole, and regardless of how much she's trying to hide the fact she has been crying, I can see pain in her eyes. All I want to do is hold her in my arms and make everything better, even though I have no clue what's going on.

When Raegan makes the motion to leave, I don't hesitate. I follow her outside to her truck. She turns when she gets to the driver's seat, and I move as close to her as possible. The fact we've been in the same house, and I have barely been able to touch her has been driving me crazy.

"Ummm," escapes her lips as mine begin to move from hers.

"'Ummm' is right. Raegan, I don't want you to leave, but I'm sure this isn't the best place for this."

"I think you might be right." She winks.

Taking every ounce of willpower I have within me, I kiss the tip of her nose and tell her I'll see her before school starts, but I'm shocked when she tells me she won't be there. I have a feeling she's keeping something from me, but only time will tell.

CHAPTER 20

Raegan

I drive slowly to the farm. Between my blurred vision and the nausea growing in my stomach, I'm terrified of what I'm going to face tomorrow. I know Grandaddy said it's going to be okay, but I'm scared to death I'm going to lose the most important person in my life.

As I arrive back at the farm, I'm greeted by Hank lying on the porch. I smile, but come to think of it, he's not been around the past couple of days. *I swear, if he's knocked up that mutt down the road, Grandaddy is gonna shoot him.* I call for him as I make my way to the porch.

"Hank, please, tell me you've not been up to what I think," I say to him. As he begins to wag his tail uncontrollably, I know I'm right. "He's gonna kill ya, ya know?" He barks. I just love him. I take a few minutes to show him some loving before I go inside to get ready to call it a night. Physically, mentally, and emotionally, I'm a mess.

Walking inside the house, I try to push tomorrow away from my mind and go to bed, but I'm unable to shake my worry. Instead, I decide a little ride around the farm is exactly what I need. I leave Grandaddy a note and walk to the shed to crank up the four-wheeler and take a ride around the beautiful farm.

As the semi-cool breeze hits my face, the wind whips my hair. I push everything to the back of my mind. I focus on driving as fast as possible and cover every inch of the farm. Once I see the creek approaching, memories of my time with Emmett replace the hopeless feeling in the pit of my stomach, and I smile as happy tears stream down my face.

The sun is well beyond setting when I make my way back to the house, and I see that Grandaddy has returned. After I park the four-wheeler, I go inside and join him in the kitchen for a quick bite to eat.

"Looks like you had a good ride tonight?" he asks.

"Yeah, I did. I think I covered every inch out there."

Trying not to put it off any longer, I ask the inevitable, "So, what time do we need to be there tomorrow?" I attempt to hide the fear in my voice.

"I'm supposed to be there at nine for a little more blood work, and my appointment is at ten. Now, Sunshine, you don't have to go. I'm fine to go by myself." He tries to insist.

"I know what you're tryin' to do. I know you *can* go by yourself, but I'm *not* lettin' you," I say forcefully.

"Easy, Sunshine. I know you well enough to know you're not lettin' this go. What are you missin' tomorrow mornin'?" he asks.

"Just physics and English. I'm good, though," I say.

"Well, I just wanted to make sure you weren't missin' anything too important."

I drop my food onto my plate. "Are you serious right now?" He looks at me like I've completely lost it. "Nothing, and I mean *nothing,* is more important than you. Stop acting like this isn't a big deal. It's *your* life. It's precious to me, and I'm gonna be there. I don't care if it's not a big deal when we walk out of there tomorrow, but if it is, you aren't going to be there alone."

He doesn't say anything, but I see a glimmer of a tear form in his eyes. "Grandaddy, I'm sorry, but it's the truth. How can you always be positive about everything?" I sincerely question.

"Sunshine, I want you to listen to me. I've lived a great life. I have you, and you keep my world spinning. No matter what happens tomorrow, we will keep on keepin' on. God won't give us more than we can bear, but if the doctor says he's got this, then there's no reason to get yourself worked up. You are the strongest girl I know, so quit worrying, and let's see what tomorrow holds." Just like that, Grandaddy shoots it straight, and I know he's telling the truth.

After we finish eating, we enjoy the Atlanta Braves on TV before going to bed. "Gosh, we just need to turn 'em off. This is horrible!" he says, and I giggle.

"Now, you know you love them, even if they aren't hittin' much this year. We've gotta go to a game this summer. Whatcha think?" I say.

"I think that sounds like a plan, and if that pitcher starts throwing like a pansy, I'm gonna tell 'em."

"Night, Grandaddy," I say as I continue to giggle down the hall.

Once I'm inside my room, the silence allows doubt to seep back into my mind, and I listen to my favorite Miranda Lambert album on my iPod. As I place my earbuds into my ears, I turn up the volume and crawl into bed. Somewhere between "Me and Charlie Talking" and "Mama, I'm Alright," I fall asleep.

Sometime within the night, I pull the earbuds from my

ears and pull the covers snuggly up to my chin. When the alarm sounds before dawn, I groggily make my way out of the covers and place my feet onto the cool wooden floor. Today begins like any other day, but it's different in the same. I make my rounds on the farm, but instead of rushing to school, I move as slow as a snail toward Cleveland Hematology and Oncology.

Emmett

When Raegan drives away, it is almost as if she is running from something. I try to brush it off, but I can't. There's something that takes over when you care about someone. It's something that makes you want to move the biggest mountain to make everything better for that person.

As I begin to walk back inside, Mr. Lowery meets me in the driveway, yet again.

"We've gotta stop meetin' this way," he says with a smile, but the smile soon fades when he sees the worry in my eyes.

"Is she okay?" I question.

"She will be. Just know when she cares about someone, she doesn't let them go, no matter what it might look like." He doesn't say anything else, but that leaves the wheels spinning in my head. I'm not sure exactly what he's talking about, but I'm going to find out. I'm certain that Cole knows exactly what's going on. I make my way up to his room, but when I hear the shower running, I know I'm going to have to wait to see what is going on with Raegan.

CHAPTER 21

Raegan

"Sunshine, you barely ate," Grandaddy says.

"I'm not really hungry," I respond as I move the eggs around my plate. He leaves it at that. As he glances down at his watch, I know time is ticking like a bomb about to explode.

"I guess we better get going," he says. We walk to his truck, and I climb in the passenger seat. The ride to the doctor's office isn't that far, but when we pull into the parking lot, and I see the words written on the side, my insides begin to quiver. "Sunshine, it's gonna be fine. We'll be outta here in no time." I smile, and we exit the truck.

The front doors slide open as we near the entrance, and the smell of sterilization takes over my nose. *Yuck! Why do all doctors' offices have to smell like a crazy kinda clean?* I walk with Grandaddy to the receptionist, and she points him toward the lab.

"Sunshine, I'll be right back. Just wait out here," he says, and I nod as I take a seat and watch *The View* on TV. *At least it takes my mind off where I am at the moment. Whoopi Goldberg is freakin' hilarious!* After they finish, Grandaddy comes out to join me.

His arm is covered with a piece of nursing tape and a cotton ball. "It didn't hurt. No worries," he assures me as he glances up at the TV. "Gosh darnit! We missed Kelly this mornin'. You know, that show was so much better with Regis." My Grandaddy is always honest.

After about fifteen minutes, the nurse calls him back. I look at him, waiting for the okay to follow. He reaches out his hand, and I stand as we walk back to the exam room. The nurse checks his vital signs and tells him Dr. Charles will be in shortly. While we wait, we don't say much, and I can't quit messing with my nails.

When a light knock taps on the door, I stop fidgeting and put on a brave face. Dr. Charles is a middle-aged, slightly overweight man with a thick Southern drawl.

"Mr. Lowery," he states as he shakes his hand, and then he turns to me as Grandaddy introduces me. "Nice to meet you, Raegan," he says before taking a seat on the little round mobile stool.

He looks at the chart in his hands for a minute before he places it onto the small desk. The look on his face is hard to read, and the wait is killing me. I just want to scream for him to tell us already.

"Mr. Lowery." He stops speaking because Grandaddy asks him to call him Dover. "Dover, when we met last week, we discussed your options. When people reach a certain age, their white blood cell count can change drastically without any reason. It's extremely common."

"Yes, you said basically a pill would fix it."

"Correct." He pauses. "Dover, your blood work this morning shows something different." *Different? Different as in good or bad?* "Your white blood cell count isn't like the previous type of leukemia we were discussing. Instead, it is Acute Myeloid Leukemia. Dover, I hate to have to tell you this, but it's an aggressive type of cancer."

My world completely stops as I look at my grandaddy's face. A look of worry and anger engulf him. He tries to remain calm, but there's no use.

"Doc, I thought you said a pill would fix this? I don't have time for this," he says with aggravation in his tone.

"Dover, I understand, but you have one major factor going for you." Grandaddy looks at him and waits. "Other than your white blood cell count, you are healthy. You don't have high blood pressure or cholesterol. You take a vitamin every day and nothing else. You are in excellent shape, and with that being said, I believe you will do well with a treatment program geared for younger adults."

Grandaddy looks from me to the doctor. "Okay, tell me how this is going to work." Dr. Charles explains the different treatment options to Grandaddy. I try to listen, but my world is spinning out of control.

"Raegan. Raegan," Grandaddy says as my mind continues to race.

"Sorry, Grandaddy," I say, completely oblivious to the conversation they had been engaged in after I realized chemotherapy was involved.

"Do you understand what I'm agreeing to?" he asks.

"Yes, you're gonna take a very strong type of chemotherapy," I tell him, and both he and Dr. Charles' expression changes.

"No, Raegan, I'm not going to take any treatment." Right then anger flares within my soul. I stand and walk out of the exam room and straight toward the truck. To say I'm mad is an understatement. *How can he do this to me? How can he leave me when I'm already alone? He can't give up. I need him.* I open the truck door, climb inside, slam the door, and scream to the top of my lungs. Not that it helps take away the pain, but at least I feel better. I replace my screams with uncontrollable sobs, and I don't even realize we are on our way back home.

As we pull up to the house, I push away the tears. I'm furious with my grandaddy, but I know deep down he has a reason for everything. When he puts the truck into park, he turns to look at me.

"Sunshine, I know you don't understand, but I did what I thought was right. You are almost an adult, and I've lived a good life, but after you walked out of that room, I realized I needed to try for you. So, I'm going to try. I'm gonna try for you, Sunshine." Instantly, my fear is replaced by hope. I grab Grandaddy and hug him, never wanting to let him go.

Emmett

I pull my phone from my pocket, again. Not a word from Raegan. I hope everything is okay. From not hearing anything from her last night, and her not being at school, I think I'm going to go crazy.

When I make my way to the table for lunch, I scan the cafeteria to see if she is with Jordyn. I realize quickly she's not when I see Jordyn walk inside alone and take a seat beside Ridge.

"Have you heard from Raegan this mornin'?" I ask.

"Just earlier to say she was gonna be late. I'm sure it's nothin'," she implies.

As I take out my phone and begin to text her, I see her making her way toward our table. She sees me and smiles. I stand to meet her as she approaches.

"I was startin' to wonder 'bout you," I say.

"Nothin' to worry 'bout. You know, I've never understood why doctors want us to be on time, but yet they aren't," she says, and that is the truth. "So, what's been goin' on this mornin'?"

"Nothin' much, except I've missed you like crazy," I say as I pull her in for a hug, and if I didn't know any better, she is holding on to me like her life depends on it, and then she tells me she missed me more. I could listen to her sweet words from now until forever, and it wouldn't ever get old.

After lunch, I walk her to class. I observe how she always speaks to everyone that looks her way, no matter if they are popular or not. She is never too busy for anyone, and when I have to leave her in the doorway of her next class, I stare as she takes her seat. When she catches me, I grin and turn to head to class.

CHAPTER 22

Raegan

When Emmett tells me he missed me like crazy, I feel like the biggest liar around. I can't believe I made it to school, let alone not look like complete crap, and here he is telling me he missed me. *What kind of person keeps a secret like this? But, it's what Grandaddy wants, and that's what he will get. I always keep my promises, and this one might eat me alive.*

On the way to third block, it seems as if everyone is looking my way. I always speak to everyone, but today, it's about to drain the life out of me. I'd have loved to have stayed home and spent time with Grandaddy, but he insisted I go on to school. After he told me he was going to at least try one type of treatment, I knew I could face today, and I'm glad to know the only face I wanted to see was waiting for me to arrive.

When the bell rings for the end of the day, I hurry to practice, but not before calling the house to see if Grandaddy is okay. He is out of breath, but it is from trying to grab the phone in time before it quit ringing. He seems to be his normal self, but deep down, I can't help but wonder if he is as scared as me.

After practice, I head home, and our night is uneventful

except for one conversation. Grandaddy and I talk in depth about what his plan of action will be, and when it will start. He has chosen to take a form of oral chemotherapy, instead of the IV type, for now. He wants to see if it will help lower his white blood cell count, and Dr. Charles feels this is a good way to start. He begins taking the pills tomorrow, and I can't help but wish that Cole were back working on the farm so he could keep a check on him. *Cole. I think I'll call him later.*

Once the dishes are done, I get ready for another day of school. When I'm ready to call it a night, I call Cole. He answers on the first ring.

"Hello?" he answers, and I now realize I should have called him earlier.

"Hey, Cole, you're not asleep, are you?" I ask, suddenly regretting calling him since he's not recuperated yet.

"Nah, I'm starting to feel more like myself, but Dad and Emma are insisting I take it easy. I meant to call you earlier, but didn't know if Emmett was with you or anything."

"I haven't seen him since school. Has Grandaddy called you yet?" I ask.

"Actually, he came by after you went to school. I should have called you earlier, but I know you like your time to sort out things," he says. "Are you okay, Rae? I mean, *really* okay?" There is tenderness in his voice.

I try to force back the tears, but they stream down my face as I speak as honestly as possible. "Cole, he wasn't even gonna try to get better. How could he do that to me? I'd be lost without him, and that's exactly what would've happened if he didn't try."

"Rae, I think he didn't know what to do, but I know he was tore up when he got here. I've never seen him like that. You are his world, and when you walked out of that room, he knew he had to fight it for you."

"I just don't want to lose him. Cole, if he gets sick, and I'm not home, what am I gonna do? He doesn't want us to tell."

Cole doesn't say anything for a moment. When he finally speaks, he asks, "When does he start taking the medicine?"

"Tomorrow."

"I'll see if Dad will let me visit tomorrow. I promise not to lift a finger, but at least someone will be there. Plus, I'm dying to get out of this house." *Dying. Not exactly the word I wanted to hear.*

"Thanks, Cole, you're the best," I say as we hang up.

Emmett

As I walk to my room from getting a shower, I hear Cole talking on the phone. It's obvious he's talking to Raegan. I'm glad they are close, but the tone in his voice is filled with concern. I don't really know where Raegan went today, but I'm positive Cole has an idea.

After I know he is off the phone, I wait a few minutes before I pay him a visit. It's time to get some answers.

"What's up, Emmett?" he asks.

"Well, that's what I was hoping you could tell me." His face looks like I've caught him red-handed.

"Whatcha mean?" he tries to say without a falter in his voice, but I can still hear it.

I take a seat in the desk chair in the corner. "What's going on with Raegan? Whatever it is, I can handle it, but I know she lied to me today. I just know she did, and I know she's talked to you."

Cole looks like a deer caught in the headlights. He tries to shake off the topic, but I'm not letting this go. If she needs me, I'm going to be there.

"Look, Emmett. This isn't my story to tell."

Rage consumes me. I stand and begin pacing the floor. I know Cole is a man of his word, and he's not going to tell me. So, if he's not, I'm going to find out somehow.

"Cole, please, tell me she's okay. I know if you made a promise, you're not gonna tell me, but at least give me that much."

"*She* is fine," he says with added emphasis on the word 'she'. *Wonder what that means?* Then, it hits me. Mr. Lowery.

The look on my face must confirm to Cole that I understand. He gives me a head nod. "I'm gonna talk my dad into letting me visit the farm tomorrow while she's at school. Someone needs to be there with him."

"Can you tell me why?" I ask, no longer full of rage but fear for both Raegan and Mr. Lowery.

"I can't. It's not my place, but you can't let her know you know," he says.

"I won't," I vow. "Thanks, Cole, I've been driving myself crazy."

As I start to leave, Cole stops me. "Emmett, she cares about you more than anyone I've ever seen, but get ready, because when *this* storm hits, it's gonna be a rough one."

I acknowledge his comment and make my way to my room. *How am I going to act like I don't know?* I pull out a notebook from the side table and write exactly how I feel about her.

CHAPTER 23

Raegan

For the next two months, things continue as planned. I go to school, fall further and further head over heels for Emmett, and Grandaddy is doing great. Not one person has noticed anything odd about Grandaddy or me. I'm exhausted and running on empty. Today, Cole started working at half capacity on the farm. It's not a full tank of gas, but I'll take it!

Last month at Grandaddy's appointment, Dr. Charles felt the pills were doing their job maintaining his white blood count, but not lowering it. I knew within my soul that another plan of action was going to have to happen, and this one was going to be harder to hide from the people of Pleasant Hill. He agreed to give the pills one more month, and then he would start IV chemotherapy.

"Sunshine, Cole said he'd go with me today, so you don't have to miss school," Grandaddy says as we eat breakfast. I give him the *you can't be serious* look. "Dr. Charles knows what he's doing. He explained it to us last month. It's either we keep this going, or I try something new."

I know he's telling the truth. I want to go with him, but I also know he wants me to keep living my life. School is important to both of us, and if he does have to try the other kind of chemotherapy, I might need to save my absences.

"Tell Cole to text me what y'all decide as soon as you leave," I say, not wanting to admit my defeat.

"Will do, Sunshine. Now, hurry up. You're gonna be late. I love you," he says as he hugs me goodbye.

"I love you, too, Grandaddy," I reply as Cole enters the house.

"Mornin', Rae," he says.

"Hey, Cole."

"So, you're really gonna let us do this ourselves?" he questions.

"You know there's no arguing with him when he's made up his mind, and it is made up," I answer, and Cole laughs.

"You do recognize you're as stubborn as him?" I tilt my head, place my hands on my hips, and smile. "Yeah, ya know. What do I have to do to make you happy in all of this?" he asks.

"I expect a text as soon as you are leaving. I'm gonna be one bottle of nerves, and I have to know what is decided."

"Got it. Now, go. You're gonna be late," he says.

Emmett

As the warning bell rings, I know I have to get moving from my truck. *Where the heck is she?* I pull out my phone and text her quickly. She doesn't reply, which makes me worry. Knowing I have to get to class, I start to make my way inside. I glance over my shoulder, and there is still no sign of her.

After taking my seat in class, I check my phone again

and text Cole.

> Me: Where's Rae?
> Cole: On her way
> Me: Thanks

I place my phone back into my pocket and get ready to take a few notes. There's no way I can focus, though. I stare at the clock, and every bad scenario runs through my mind. *That's it! I can't take it anymore!* I raise my hand and wait for the teacher to acknowledge me before I excuse myself from the classroom and start to wander the halls.

I start by walking by her classroom, and I don't see her. I continue to roam the halls, giving up on the idea that I have any clue where she might be when my phone buzzes in my pocket.

> Raegan: I'm here. Had 2 handle something
> this morning.
> Me: K U n class yet?
> Raegan: No
> Me: Meet me at ur locker
> Raegan: K

I really don't know what I'm thinking or what she's going to tell me, but as her locker comes into view, I see her smiling face making her way toward me. All apprehensions disappear when I'm in her presence.

When I get within arms' reach, I take her and pull her close to me. "You had me sweatin' bullets this mornin'. I thought something had happened to ya."

She pulls back and looks into my eyes. "Nah, just runnin' behind, and then Cole had to inform me of a few things on the farm before I left."

Pushing her hair behind her ear, I look into her eyes, and I can sense she's lying to me. Even with the lies, I know she's trying to protect me from whatever is going on with her granddaddy. I just wish she'd tell me. I brush my lips quickly against hers, and we go our separate ways to class.

CHAPTER 24

Raegan

While sitting in class, all I can think about is Grandaddy and how I continue to hide this from Emmett. Since the day he walked into my life, we've grown closer, but I know we want to see how this plays out. I know I need to trust him with this, but I don't want him to feel sorry for me.

When the bell rings, I hurry to my locker and check my phone. *Nothing.* I put it back into my pocket and grab my textbooks before heading toward second block. As I'm entering the doorway, I feel a vibration in my pocket. Once I'm seated at my desk, I check to see if it's Cole. It is. Unsure of how I will react, I ask Mrs. Horn if I can run to the restroom. When she excuses me, I make a beeline for the bathroom, shut the stall door, and open the text.

Cole: It's still the same.

Taking a minute to process what I've read, my mind begins to race. *Still the same? That means they are trying the hard stuff this go round.* Without another thought, I call Cole.

"Hey, Rae."

"Hey, when are they going to start?" I ask, forcefully

holding back the tears.

"Monday. He's right here. Do you wanna talk to him?"

"Sure." I hear Cole pass Grandaddy the phone.

"Hey, Sunshine," he says. "Shouldn't you be in class?"

"Yeah, but I needed to be alone a minute," I admit quietly.

"It's gonna be fine. Cole, Dr. Charles, and I worked out a schedule. Hopefully, it will only take a few treatments, and I'll be good as new."

"I hope so," I say as someone comes into the bathroom. "I better go. I'll be home as soon as I can today. Love you." I hang up quickly so whoever came in doesn't hear me.

When I open the door, I come face-to-face with Jordyn. "Hey, girl."

"Who were you talkin' to, and *why* are you missin' class?" she probes with a little more attitude than usual.

"Grandaddy. He had a question about the finances at the farm before he went to the bank," I say as guilt eats away at me.

"I'm not buying it, Rae."

"Well, it's the truth."

"I'm callin' you out.. You've been up to something for weeks now. I don't know what it is, but just know, nothing is too bad that you can't talk to me about it. I'm your best friend, remember?"

Grief washes over my body. "I know, but that's it. I know I can tell you anything. I've just been really stressed out lately with the farm, especially since Cole's been out."

"Look, I don't know what's going on, but come here," she says as she waves her arms toward me for a hug.

"Thanks, J, and thanks for not asking questions."

"You're welcome. Now, let's get back before someone comes lookin' for us," she states as she loops my arm through hers.

I'm thankful to have Jordyn in my life. She knows me well enough to know what buttons to push and when to run the other direction. I love her for it.

"So, I heard there's a party this Saturday. Do you wanna go?" she asks.

"J, there's a party every Saturday night." I laugh.

"Yeah, but you haven't been to one since Emmett showed up."

"What can I say? He's where it's at." I smirk.

"You little hussy!" She grins, and we part ways back to class.

Emmett

I know I am overstepping my boundaries when I do it, but I can't resist. I have to know what's going on. As soon as I am out of eyesight from Raegan, I call Cole, but there isn't an answer. *What in the world?* I send him a text and still nothing. *What is it with no one answering me today?*

Brushing it off, I make my way to class. At lunch, Raegan is her bubbly self, but our conversation almost seems like it's on autopilot. I want to get her alone and find out what is going on, but I know if she finds out I know, she's going to hate me... and Cole. I can't let her push us away, because she is going to need us at some point.

After lunch, I finally get a text from Cole. It appears his lips are sealed shut, but I'm going to find out what is going on. This day isn't going anywhere close to how I'd planned, and I just want to get out of here as fast as possible. The only thing stopping me is Raegan. If I walked out right now, no one but her would really care if I were gone. It might even make a few people, like Jace, happy, but I can't leave her without telling her. She'd freak out, just like I did this morning.

When the afternoon bell rings, I wait on her at her locker. She smiles, and I want to hold her in my arms and demand she tell me what she's hiding. Instead, I hold her close, inhale her scent, and pray it will all go away.

CHAPTER 25

Raegan

As my truck makes it way down the drive, I see Cole, Grandaddy, and Hank sitting on the front porch. I smile at the three of them as I head their way. Those two men have been what keeps me hopeful in this world and make life worth living.

"Hey, y'all," I say as I make my way to them and take a seat beside them. "Please, tell me y'all haven't been front porch sitting while I've been in class all day."

"We wish," Cole says smartly.

"Boy, you know you don't have to work here," Grandaddy says flatly. *What's Cole's deal?*

"I'm just kiddin', Uncle Dover. I wouldn't want to work anywhere else."

"Good, 'cause I need ya here bright and early in the mornin'." I try to refrain from laughing, but it's no use. "Sunshine, why are you laughin'? I gotta have you, too." I stop mid-giggle. I've never seen him like this, and I look at Cole for direction.

"Grandaddy, is everything okay?" I ask.

He exhales a big puff of air. "Yeah, it's all right, or it will be. It's just been a long day, and we've got to get this hay baled before Monday. I can't have that weighing on my shoulders when I'm sitting in a doctor's office with a needle in my arm." *Oh God, this isn't good. He rarely uses four-letter words!*

"No worries, we got this. Right, Cole?" I say in his direction.

"Heck, yeah. Y'all want me to see if Emmett will pitch in tomorrow?" he asks.

In unison, both Grandaddy and I exclaim, "No!"

"Y'all, he doesn't know, and we could use an extra hand," Cole insinuates. I look at Grandaddy, and he asks what I want to do.

"I guess, but I swear, Cole, if he figures out anything, I'm gonna beat the shit outta ya!" I cover my mouth from surprise of what just popped out. Both Grandaddy and Cole look at me like I've lost it. "Sorry, it just kinda slipped. But, I've had to watch every move I've made for the past couple of months, and if he finds out now, what's been the point in keeping it a secret?" I say bluntly.

"Sunshine, it's not Emmett I'm worried about. It's everyone else in this town."

"Well, you told me not to tell, and I haven't. I've lied to everyone I care about, and I plan on keeping it that way until this is just water under the bridge."

After my rant on the front porch, I make my way inside to try to calm down. As I pace the floor, I hear footsteps approaching. Ignoring whomever it might be, I walk to the fridge and pour myself a glass of cold sweet tea. *Maybe it will help.* I turn and see Cole standing there with his arms crossed. He's definitely pissed.

"Rae, what up?" he asks.

"Whatcha mean? I just told y'all what I was thinkin'. That's all."

"If that's what you wanna tell yourself. Listen, you do know that if you told Emmett, he would understand."

"Understand? He might, but I'm not gonna."

"Why do you gotta be such a stubborn jackass. Get over it. Whatever you're thinkin', get over it!" he yells, and I stomp past him and up to my room to throw a hissy fit and a pity party all-in-one.

After an hour or so, there's a light knock on my door. "Sunshine." I hear Grandaddy say just above a whisper. "Can I come in?"

"Yeah," I answer as I wipe my eyes and attempt to ignore the fact I just acted like a preschooler.

When he opens the door, I can see the concern in his eyes. He takes a few steps, reaches my bed, and takes a seat beside me.

"Sunshine, I never should have asked you to keep this secret, but we all know that with one lie comes another. As hard as it is for me to say this, I thought this was going to be a simple fix, but it's turning out to be the complete opposite. If you want to tell Emmett and the rest of this Podunk town, I'm with ya. I love you too much to watch it eat you alive."

"Grandaddy, I don't want to tell. I don't want their pity. Let's just see what happens," I say.

"Are you sure?" he asks once more.

"I'm positive."

He pats my leg before he stands, tells me he loves me, and then asks about my plans for tonight. I tell him I had planned on hanging out with him, and he tells me it's crazy to wanna spend time with an old man. He insists I pick up my phone and call Emmett to take me out on the town. I smile while shaking my head. *I don't think I can love anyone more than I love him right now.*

When he leaves, I call Emmett to see what he's up to.

"Hey, Beautiful," he answers.

"Hey, whatcha up to?" I ask.

"Not much, I just got finished talkin' to Cole. It looks like I'll be at your beck an' call tomorrow, but you know what?"

"What?"

"I might actually like it."

"Ohmygosh! Really? I have to say; I get the better end of that deal. You all hot and sweaty minus a shirt. Yeah, I'll take it."

"You ain't right. So, really, what's up?" Silence.

"Ummm, I was gonna just hang out with Grandaddy, but he's told me that was a negative tonight. You think he's gotta woman friend he's tryin' to hide?" *Where did that come from?*

Emmett bursts out laughing. "I doubt that, but if he did, who would it be?"

"Ohmygosh, I can't believe we're even talkin' 'bout this."

"No, really, if you could see him with anyone, who would it be?"

Never in my life have I thought about him with anyone other than Mawmaw. "I don't know... it's weird to think like that."

"What about Pearl Allen?"

"No! She's too prim and proper. He'd need someone like Agnes Berrier. She's like Southern Belle meets redneck. Ya know, classy when needed and red any other time."

"Now that you put it that way, I totally see it."

"Anyway! So, the reason I called was to see what you

had planned tonight."

"Raegan Lowery, are you askin' me out on a date?" he asks with a fake gasp in his tone.

"Why, yes, Mr. Bridges, I am."

"Are you payin'?" he asks with a laugh.

"Whatever works for me," I say, and he quickly informs me that he will be paying and picking me up at seven. *Crap! It's already after five!*

I let Grandaddy know I'm going out with Emmett, and he smiles. I hurry upstairs to get ready. I crank up a little Luke Bryan on my iPod and get ready as fast as possible.

At ten until seven, I see Emmett making his way up the driveway. Grandaddy tells me to be careful, and I walk outside to meet Emmett. I'm not giving him a moment's time with Grandaddy. I'll wait until tomorrow to wait on the classy yet redneck jokes to start.

Emmett hops out of the truck as he sees me making my way toward the truck. He's standing there in a pair of Rock 'n Roll jeans and a fitted tee. Every muscle in his body is evident, and I just want to reach out and touch him. This becomes a reality when he meets me on the passenger side.

Wrapping my arms around his neck, he pulls me in closely and lightly kisses my lips. "He's watchin', ya know," Emmett says as his eyes point toward the house.

"Yeah, I know," I reply as I kiss his nose and pull away to get into the truck. He just shakes his head. As he makes his way around, I observe that fine specimen of a guy in front of me. *How'd I get so lucky?* When he slides inside the truck, I cut a glance toward him, and he smiles and places his hand around my neck, giving me the kind of kiss I've been waiting for.

CHAPTER 26

Raegan

"So, where are we goin'?" I ask him.

He looks at me like he's clueless. "You asked me out, remember?" He then laughs when I'm speechless.

"How 'bout let's go to the city for a nice meal and then see where the night leads?" he suggests.

I quickly begin to rethink my attire, but realize he's in jeans, so there's no need to worry about a five-star, top of the tower meal. "Sounds good to me. Whatcha thinkin'?" I ask.

"Maybe Cheddar's?" he asks.

"Sounds perfect!" We make our way out of Pleasant Hill and toward "the city" as we call it, but it's not like a big metropolis. It's more like a bigger redneck town with lots of shopping, restaurants, and a place to cruise on Saturday nights.

After we pull into the parking lot, I wait for Emmett to open my door. I slide out of the truck, and he laces his fingers in mine as we enter.

Walking into Cheddar's is like going on vacation. The décor makes you feel as if you just walked out of a hotel room and into an exotic location. There are waterfalls, beautiful copper fixtures, and intricate rock details. After a short wait, we make our way to a table near the aquarium and glance at the menu as the waiter takes our drink order.

Our meal is filled with flirting, fun, laughter, and pushing limits. When we both can't eat another bite, the waiter brings the check. After Emmett pays, we walk outside. The night air is damp and cool, and I can feel my hair starting to frizz.

"Em, I got an idea. You wanna hear?" He looks at me with question in his eyes.

"Of course."

"Let's go out to the train tracks behind the Thompsons' place. Maybe we can catch one coming by."

"Sounds like a plan to me," he says with a half-grin.

During the half-hour ride back to Pleasant Hill, I try to get as close to him as I can. *Dang this console!* Emmett looks my way and smirks, and if I didn't know any better, I'd think he was thinking the exact same thing.

As we approach the Thompson property, Emmett finds a place to park the truck off the road and hidden from any cars that might drive by. We don't want the 5-0 called on us. Once he's satisfied with the spot, he grabs a flashlight, and we make our way through the field toward the pond. We are greeted by the sound of bullfrogs, gnats, and a few horses.

As I swat away the gnats, Emmett laughs.

"What's so funny, Em?" I ask.

"I never thought I'd have to keep away gnats. I always thought it would just be Jace."

"You are too funny, and there's no need to swat away Jace. I think he's finally taken the hint," I say as we begin to walk around the pond and toward the tracks on the hill.

As we reach the tracks, I motion for Emmett to come on.

With the flashlight lighting the way, I use the track as a balance beam while he follows me.

"Em, do you wanna play Truth or Dare?" I ask as I continue to walk.

"Sure, you can go first," he says.

"Em. Truth or dare?"

"Dare," he says confidently.

"I dare you to do a toe touch."

"Are you serious?" He stops on the tracks. "Hold this," he says as he hands me the light. "Now, if I rip these jeans, you're gonna owe me." He rubs his hands together like he's making a wish, and then he looks at me and jumps. It's not anywhere close to a toe touch, but it makes me laugh. "My turn," he declares as he takes the light from me. "Rae, truth or dare?"

"Dare," I say assertively.

"I dare you to sing to me."

Taking a step toward him, I inhale deeply and sing "Are You Gonna Kiss Me or Not?"

"Keep goin'," is all he says as he takes a step closer to me. As I finish the song, he moves my hair behind my ear.

"Em, truth or dare?" I ask, inches separating us.

"Dare."

"I *dare* you to kiss me." He smiles and pulls me into him, and our lips do the talking. As our kisses deepen, the faint sound of a train whistle looms in the distance. I open my eyes and see Emmett has heard it as well.

"Rae, truth or dare?" he asks.

"Dare."

"I dare you a round of chicken on the tracks."

"You're on."

Emmett

I know the moment I make that dare, I'm gonna lose, but this game of chicken is going to be a little different. As soon as she agrees, I pull her lips back onto mine and wait for the sound of the train.

As the train approaches, Raegan acts as if it is invisible. *She's so stubborn, and that makes her so freakin' hot.* She continues to press her lips to mine while her hands roam my body, making concentrating on the approaching train more difficult.

"Not thinkin' 'bout chickening out, are ya?" she whispers into my ear.

"No," I say as the ground below begins to tremor, and one single headlight lights the way. Inside, I'm about to freak out. I don't want to die, and she's sure not going to. As I pick her up off the ground, she wraps her legs around me, and my body tenses as we stare into each other's eyes while the whistle continuously blows and the ground feels as if it's about to crumble beneath us. When my heart can't handle it anymore, I break my stare and move us from the track. Once we are safely off the tracks, I attack her lips yet again not wasting another minute. I'm not sure if it's the fear of what we could have lost, but in this moment, I can't get enough of her. As I continue to get lost in her, I'm brought back to the present as the train rushes by and the rush of air makes me realize just how much I need her.

"Rae, truth or dare."

"Truth," she says.

"What's your favorite memory of me from before I left?"

CHAPTER 27

Raegan

What do I say? I have to answer truthfully. I try not to grin like a crazy person when I think about it, but I can't help it. "When you brought me the stuffed bunny. That's my favorite memory of you." I say as Emmett continues to hold me in his arms.

"Why?" he asks, and I know he's not following the rules.

"The day you brought me that bunny was the day I realized that someone other than Grandaddy truly cared about me. I knew life would get better, and it reminds me every time I look at it."

As I slide down his body, Emmett stands there, stunned. "You still have it?" he asks.

"I do."

"Raegan, there's a reason things happen in this world, and I have no doubt all those years ago was part of the plan. I just can't believe you kept it." He says as he brushes my hair behind my ear.

"It's always been a reminder of what happened with my parents, how you graciously gave like only a child can do, and how I never wanted to forget you… ever," I say as I look into his eyes.

"Over the years, I wondered if you kept it or just tossed it into the yard sale pile. I can remember going with my mom to pick it out. You were so crazy over Thumper, I knew the moment I saw it, you had to have it."

"You're right. I had to have *it*, Em," I say as I take a step toward him. "It led me to you." I place my hand on his cheek and bring my lips to his.

Emmett scoops me into his arms and walks to his truck. He turns on the radio, it begins to play a slow country song. As I lay in his arms in the bed of his truck, he begins to kiss the side of my neck as his hands roam my body. My body shivers, and I know it's time to cross a line that I can never come back from. Sitting up, I smile at him and bite the side of my lip. He takes the hem of my shirt and begins pull it above my head. Emmett looks at me with his eyes full of desire. "Are you sure, Rae?" He asks.

"I've never been so sure of anything in my life."

After giving myself completely to Emmett, I know that I have fallen head over heels in love with him. As he holds me in his arms and we look up into the moonlit sky, I realize I am going to have to tell him about Grandaddy. The question is when.

"Em, do you ever feel like everything in your world is out of control?" I ask as I prop up on my elbow.

"I used to before I moved back here, but that's life. It's out of our control. All we can do is hang on for the ride and hope we survive." *Survive.* The word hits me hard.

I push away the thoughts and ask him, "How'd I get so lucky?"

"I think we're both pretty lucky, if you ask me," he says

and then pulls me on top of him.

*****

Saturday morning arrives faster than I would have liked, but my first thought is that I get to spend the majority of it with Emmett—hot, sweaty muscles, and no shirt—or at least this is how I picture the day.

After tossing on old clothes, I take my Braves ball cap and pull my hair through the hole on the way down the stairs.

"Mornin', Sunshine," Grandaddy greets me as he sits at the table reading the newspaper while drinking his coffee and eating breakfast.

"Mornin'," I say as I pour my cup of coffee and make a plate of breakfast.

As Grandaddy puts the coffee to his mouth, a huge smile escapes his lips. "So, I take it you had a good time last night?"

Oh, Lord, does he know? Is it that obvious? "I did. What about you?" I banter back.

"Ya know, just watched the Braves and then called it a night. I'm just a regular party animal."

"I know. What am I gonna do with ya?" I giggle. "I'm gonna scarf this down and start my chores, so I can help once Cole and Em get here."

"I already got the eggs this mornin'. We'll both feed the animals and be ready to go. Take your time." It's almost as if he is soaking in these little moments we have together.

After breakfast, we make our way to the barn and feed and water the animals. Then, we sit on the porch with Hank and another cup of coffee while we wait for Cole and Emmett.

As we swing back and forth, not much is said. We just enjoy the quiet and each other's company.

"How are you today?" I ask him.

"I'm great, actually." *Great? How is he great?* "Spending

time here on the farm, working, and being with my favorite girl in the world. It doesn't get any better than this, Sunshine," he says as he puts his arms around my shoulder and hugs me tightly. He's right. It doesn't get any better than this.

When Cole's truck approaches in the distance, Grandaddy takes my cup and goes inside. I stand on the front porch with my hands in my back pockets, waiting to see Emmett emerge from the truck. *Ohmygosh!* I never knew a pair of worn-out Carhartts and a t-shirt with the sleeves cut out could look so dang good! My eyes meet his, and he smiles. Cole takes a look at both of us and shakes his head.

"Mornin', Rae," Cole says as he walks past me and into the house.

"Mornin'," I reply, but he's already inside. Emmett is standing on the first step and eye level with me.

"How are ya this mornin'?" he asks.

"I'm perfect. What 'bout you?" I say as I bite the corner of my bottom lip.

"Life couldn't get any better than right now." With those words, my heart melts, yet again. He gives me a brief kiss on my lips before we make our way inside to meet Cole and Grandaddy.

After Grandaddy gives each of us a task and what will be accomplished by the end of the day, we take our positions and work until we break for lunch. I pull out chicken salad and fresh rolls for lunch. They each eat two, and I can't help but feel my heart warm as the three men that mean the world to me are in the same room. That's when Grandaddy begins to cough uncontrollably.

"Grandaddy!" I yell. "Are you okay?" I look at Cole for direction.

Grandaddy waves us off and takes a large gulp of water.

"I'm fine. Just eatin' too fast." I let out a breath of relief. We sit about fifteen more minutes before we hit the field hard to try to finish before mid-afternoon.

When Emmett excuses himself for a moment, my eyes go straight to Grandaddy. "Are you sure you're okay?" I inquire.

"I promise. Now, Cole, I wanna have this done by three. I know y'all got better things to do than work here all day."

"Yes, sir. We got this," he says and then makes his way outside. I clean up the kitchen quickly and hurry to help them.

After the last bale of hay is lifted onto the truck, we make our way to the front porch to enjoy a glass of ice-cold sweet tea.

"So, what y'all youngins doin' tonight?" Grandaddy asks.

I look to the guys for guidance.

"I'm not sure. I know there's a field party, as usual," I reply.

"Y'all haven't been over there in a while. It's not 'cause of that Jace boy, is it?" Grandaddy questions.

"Nah, I'd just rather not, I guess, but Jordyn is about to have a fit for me to go."

"I'm game if you are," Emmett states and looks at Cole.

"Y'all know I'm not goin'," Cole says as he throws up his hands.

"Smart move, Cole!" Grandaddy laughs as he stands and says he's gonna find a spot in his recliner.

Once Grandaddy is inside, we all look at each other. "I don't know how he does all of this," Emmett says.

"It's easy, Em. This is his world. He doesn't know how *not* to work. Honestly, I think that has been what's kept him going all these years... well, and me, of course." I smirk.

"Well, Lovebirds, I'm 'bout ready to get out of these

clothes. I've got a hot date tonight," Cole says boldly. Both Emmett and I snap our heads toward him.

"With whom?" I question.

"Tammy," he responds.

"You mean that girl with whom you swear you're *just friends*?" I ask, placing the last two words in air quotes.

"That'd be the one. I guess we're not 'just friends.'" He laughs as he stands. "Emmett, you're riding with me," he says with a wink. *Ohmygosh! Cole knows!*

"Yeah, so, Rae, do you wanna go to the party tonight? Might be fun."

I ponder his question for a minute. "Sure, I wouldn't mind a little dancing by the fire," I say as I brush my hand across his chest and start to walk toward the door. He grabs it, turns me to him, and attacks my lips.

"I'll see ya at seven," he informs me as he backs away and down the steps toward Cole's truck. I wave, but not before making sure Cole has us both covered tonight. He'll give Emmett our shine before he picks me up. I need to get a little tipsy and forget the fact my world is changing.

As the screen door slams behind me, *oops,* I hear Grandaddy holler for me from the recliner.

"Yes, Grandaddy?" I ask as I enter.

"Look, I'm not blind, and I know what it's like to be a teenager. Just be careful, and if you need me, call me."

"Yes, sir," I say as I head to take a shower, so I can get supper ready before the party. After I dry my hair, I throw on a pair of yoga pants and a tank and walk downstairs to get supper cooking.

Looking in the cabinets and freezer, I have no idea what to make. After working all day, nothing sounds good except a gallon or two of water. As I continue to stare, I'm startled when

Grandaddy breaks my train of thought.

"Come on. Let's get a burger," he says.

"A'ight."

Grandaddy and I make our way to the Tasty-T for the best burgers south of the Mason- Dixon Line. As we approach the order window, he lets me order first, and then we find a picnic table to sit and eat. Even with the cool fall air, it's still nice outside.

As our order is shouted from the window, I stand to pick it up, but Grandaddy insists on getting it. I meet him halfway to grab the drinks anyway.

After Grandaddy takes the first bite, he shakes his head and says, "Um, um, um, man, that's good!" He's right; it sure is. While we eat, he talks about the farm, things he wants to get done over the next week, and then *it* happens. He starts asking questions no one *ever* wants to talk to their grandfather or any parental figure about.

"Rae, you love him, don't ya?" he asks between bites of fries.

I stare at my fries, but I might as well be honest with him, because there's no use in starting to lie now. I look Grandaddy directly in the eyes. "Yeah, I love him, but I haven't told him yet."

"I knew you fell in love with him all those years ago, but to see you both as young adults makes my heart happy. I always knew the right guy would come along to replace me."

"He's not gonna replace you! No one can!" He shakes his head again.

"Sunshine, there comes a time in every child's life where their parents are no longer the loves of their life. It's okay. In fact, I'm glad Emmett showed up when he did, even though I would like to shoot him for it, ya know?" My eyes bug out of my head. *Always keeping it real.* I try to change the subject, but he raises his hand to stop me. "I'm not going to, but I knew this day would come. I'm not saying I agree with it or like it at all. Lord knows I don't want to be a great-granddaddy anytime soon, so you take yourself to the doctor this week, missy."

I'm in complete shock, which I shouldn't be, because this is Grandaddy up one side and down the other, I reply, "Yes, sir." *Mental note: See the doctor on Monday.*

After my reply, Grandaddy goes back to talk about the Braves, and that's when I decide to plan our trip this summer.

"Grandaddy, who do you want to see the Braves play? I mean, when we go this summer?"

"I wouldn't mind seeing the Red Sox or Rangers. So, we're really gonna do this?" he states.

"Yup, we are." I pull out my phone and check the calendar. "Looks like it's gonna be the Braves versus Red Sox."

"Allll righhht!" he says, and my cup runneth over with pure happiness.

On our way back to the farm, Grandaddy and I roll down the windows and crank up the radio. When Miranda Lambert's "Over You" comes through the speakers, I let my voice do the talking.

"Man, oh, man, I'll never get tired of hearing you sing," he says.

"Well, I did learn from the best."

"Who me?" he asks as I shake my head yes. "Shoot."

"Grandaddy, you know it's the truth. Come on. Sing it for me."

He grins, and with that, he turns down the radio and sings my favorite hymn, "Amazing Grace." As his deep voice hits every note right on key, I smile at him, and when the chorus begins, I harmonize with him. We spend the remainder of the ride home singing and acting like there isn't a care in the world.

As Grandaddy puts the truck into park and turns off the ignition, he turns to look at me. "Sunshine, when something happens to me, whether it's today, tomorrow, or fifty years from now, promise me that you will sing *for* me."

Tears threaten my eyes. "I promise." After we walk into the house, I go straight to my room to get ready for the party with Emmett.

A few minutes before seven, I see Emmett's truck pulling up the driveway. I hurry to finish up my makeup, but not before Grandaddy lets him inside. I can hear them talking from my room, but can't make out a word. *Lord, please, don't let Granddaddy tell him that he knows!*

Emmett

As I start to knock on the front door, it opens mid-knock.

"Evenin', Mr. Lowery," I say.

"Evenin', Emmett. Why don't you come inside?" *Oh, crap! What is going on?* I make my way inside and he leads me to the kitchen, where I see a shotgun lying on the table. *Oh God, he knows, and I'm about to die right here in her kitchen.* "Boy, lose that look off your face. I need to have a word with you."

"Yes, sir." I remove my deer in the headlights look and then take a seat at the kitchen table with only the gun separating us.

"Do you love her?" he asks bluntly.

"Yes, sir, I do."

"That's good to know. I want to tell you something, but you can't let Sunshine know that you know. Do you understand me?"

"Yes, sir." Fear begins to envelop my body, knowing I'm

going to have to keep something from her, but this is it. I'm going to have the missing piece to the puzzle.

"I'm sick, Emmett. I have leukemia. We've been trying oral medication, but it's not working. I had originally asked Raegan and Cole not to say anything, but you need to know. Because I made her promise me, she will not tell you. I start some hard-core chemotherapy on Monday. I'm not sure how this is going to turn out, but I need to know my Sunshine will be taken care of if I'm no longer on this Earth. Do you understand what I'm tellin' you?" *Oh, no. Raegan's worst fear might come true, and she's been keeping it bottled up inside? This is crazy. How am I gonna act like I don't know the actual truth?*

"Yes, sir, I understand. I've known for some time now that she's been lying about something. I knew it was to protect you, but I didn't know why. Please, let me know if you ever need me or if there is anything I can do."

"Thank you, Emmett. I just need your word. She's loved you since you gave her that stuffed bunny. You have no idea what she's been through, and how one little gesture changed her life. I just need to know she's taken care of when I'm gone, because we know death is inevitable."

"You have my word," I say, realizing our relationship began to build long before we knew the meaning of love.

"Oh, and Emmett, I know." I have a puzzled look on my face, and then it clicks. *I'm dead!* "Just know if you make me a great-grandaddy before my time, this shotgun has your name *all* over it."

And, just like clockwork, Raegan walks into the kitchen.

CHAPTER 28

Raegan

By the look on Emmett's face, I'm not sure what Grandaddy said to him, but I think he just informed him of the knowledge he gained today over a burger. "Hey, y'all," I say. "Are you ready, Em?"

"Yeah, nice talkin' to you, Mr. Lowery," he says, and Grandaddy smirks and gives him a head nod.

I walk over to Grandaddy, give him a hug and tell him I love him, and then we are out the door. As soon as we are on the front porch, I look at him. "Are you okay?"

"Um, not exactly," he answers as I stop and face him. "You really do tell him everything, don't ya?"

"Actually, he figured it out, but I didn't deny it when he wanted confirmation."

Emmett doesn't say anything; he just takes me by the hand and leads me to his truck. As we make our way down the road, he glances my direction.

"What, Em?" I ask.

"Just curious...what did he tell you?"

"Just to be careful and not to make him a great-granddaddy before his time. Then, he told me to get on the pill or something." *How can I just spit this out like it's no big deal? It's a major big deal, and I can't believe I'm in the middle of this conversation. But, I guess if you are gonna do it, you better be responsible.*

"He said it just like that?" Emmett asks.

"Pretty close. You know he keeps it real," I say with a giggle.

"I do, all too well."

"So, are you ready for tonight?" I ask.

"You better believe it. Oh, and Cole said they were out of strawberry, so he got ya lemonade."

"Yummm. Let's get our *shine on*," I sing. Emmett looks my direction, and I can see in his eyes he loves me, and I love him.

As we approach the Phillips' farm, Emmett puts the truck into four-wheel drive and then parks beside the other vehicles. He comes around to let me out, and we make our way to the tailgate to chill with the moonshine in hand.

Emmett places his hands around my waist and picks me up to sit. Before he can back away, I place my arms around his neck.

"Em, thank you."

He looks at me, confused. "For what?"

"For loving me," I say, looking him in the eyes.

He takes a second to grasp what has just left my lips. "Raegan, I don't just love you. I'm *in* love with you."

"I'm *in* love with you, too," I say, as we are now so close I can feel his breath on my face. He leans in and brings his lips to mine. "I love you, Emmett Bridges."

"I love you, too, Raegan Lowery."

I never would have planned for that to be the moment I

told him I loved him, but it just felt right. The only thing I wish is that we would have been alone.

"Are you sure you wanna stay here?" he questions.

"Not really, but I wouldn't mind dancin' by the fire with ya later. Plus, Jordyn will kill me if I don't show."

"True," he says as he backs away and hops on the back of the truck beside me.

As other trucks continue to pile in, it doesn't take long for Jordyn and Ridge to arrive. She squeals as she runs to me. *That girl ain't right. Wonder how much she's drunk already?*

"Are you happy to see me, or is that the booze talkin'?" I ask her.

"Now, Rae! You know me better than that! I'm always glad to see my BFF. I'm just glad Emmett decided to share you tonight."

"Girl, like you'd even notice. You've been with Ridge every free moment you've had."

She thinks it over a minute and admits I'm right. "So, what's in the jar tonight?"

"Ya know…a little lemonade," I say with a mischievous wink.

"Ohhhhhh, my fav! Let me see it." I pass the jar to Jordyn, as Ridge finally catches up with her.

"Dang, slow down, baby," Ridge says as Jordyn holds up a finger, telling him to stop as she takes a few more gulps of the sweet liquid.

I try my best not to laugh, but when Emmett takes it straight from her mouth, I can't control myself.

"Hey, that's not funny!" she whines as Emmett takes the jar and partakes.

"Man. That's some good stuff right there," he says.

"My turn," I say, and Ridge follows after me. We've been

here less than thirty minutes, and the jar is well over half-gone.

The lower the sun sets, the louder the people become. As I scan the crowd, I see that Jace and his meathead friends have arrived. When he catches me looking their way, he smiles and raises a glass toward me. *Seriously? I know he's not happy for me. Oh, wait. I get it. I see his new mission approaching.* Jace has moved on to Missy Tate. She's everything I'm not, and I'm so glad. I give him a smile and return my focus to Jordyn, Ridge, and Emmett.

We spend the majority of the time catching up on what's going on, or rather, Jordyn tells us the gossip in our little town. When "Somethin' Bad" begins to echo from the speakers, I look at Jordyn, and we walk toward the fire. Ridge and Emmett look at each other and just shake their heads. I sing the Miranda Lambert portion while Jordyn takes Carrie Underwood. Before we know it, all the girls are approaching and singing right along with us. If I didn't know any better, I'd have thought the CMT Awards just rolled into Pleasant Hill at a dang field party.

When the song ends, we stay put and continue dancing and having a good time. Before long, guys are making their way to their ladies, and when Emmett's arms wrap around my waist from behind, I let my head fall back on his chest as we move to the beat of the music.

Once the music slows, Emmett spins me around to face him and doesn't let me go. I can't help but smile when I listen to the lyrics. "Raegan Lowery, I love you," he says, as he looks me dead in the eyes.

"Em, I love you, too." I crash my lips onto his while we sway to the music. We continue to dance for several more songs until I feel a gentle tap on my shoulder. I glance over to see Jace standing beside me.

"Hey, Jace, is everything okay?" I question, and Emmett

stares him down.

"Yeah, I was just curious to know if I might get a dance tonight." I look at Emmett for the answer, and he looks as if he is ready to pounce.

"What happened to Missy?" I inquire.

"Ya know, she's not half as fun to catch." I can feel Emmett's breathing increasing, and I know I can't have him in a brawl with Jace. *I know Em would win hands down.*

"Whatever, Jace. Can't you find some bimbo willing to give you a piece to dance with?"

Jace smirks, and I know whatever is about to escape from his mouth is going to be a cheap remark.

As a smirk unfolds on Jace's face, he begins to speak, "From what I understand, I heard you put out now, Miss Lowery."

"You son of a bitch!" Emmett hollers as he starts to swing at Jace.

"Come on, Big Boy. Let's see what you got." Jace laughs, ready to duke it out with him.

"Em, he's not worth it," I say calmly. When he ignores me, I yell for Ridge to help. Before I can process it, a crowd is beginning to huddle around. I never let go of Emmett, as he's ready to give Jace what's been coming to him for years. Emmett begins to hit Jace blow after blow and I'm thankful when Ridge jumps in to pull Emmett off Jace. One of the meatheads grabs Jace and helps him up. Ridge begins to push Emmett toward the truck, but when Emmett sees a chance to escape, he does, and I run after him.

As Emmett tackles Jace from behind, I scream in horror as Jace tosses him over his back and begins to make contact with Emmett's body. When Jace feels he's had enough, he backs away from Emmett, then turns to walk away. As soon as his back is turned, Emmett stands slowly and eggs Jace on once again. After another round of blows, several guys pull them off of each other, and we finally make our way to Ridge's truck.

Ridge turns to me. "Get his keys and get him outta here. Who knows what Jace will do next?"

"I'm fine to drive, Rae!" Emmett shouts.

"I'm driving. Do *not* argue with me," I say as I shove my hand into his pocket and take the keys from him.

Emmett

When Raegan took control like that, it snapped me back to reality. *Why did I do something so stupid? Jace isn't worth my time. Must be the shine talkin'. Who am I kidding? No one's gonna talk about my girl like that.*

Once we are in the truck and halfway down the hill toward the main road, I finally decide to speak.

"Rae, I'm sorry 'bout back there."

"It's fine." She says flatly.

"No, it's not. I shouldn't have let him get to me like that, but no one is going to talk about you like that... ever!"

She slams on the breaks, and I lunge forward. "Look, the question is, how does he know? It's not like I've told anyone but Grandaddy. I'm pretty sure Cole knows, too. That's what pisses me off. Please, tell me you didn't try to one-up him or something."

What in the world? Pain. That's what I feel straight to my heart. I would never hurt her. "Rae, I haven't said a word to him, I promise." I take my hand and try to touch her, but she moves it.

"Stop. I don't want to hear it right now," she says as she brings her hand up to swat mine away.

"Let me drive. I'm good," I say.

"No," she states, continuing toward the main road.

"Rae, let me drive. I don't want you to get a ticket. We drank a lot quickly tonight." She looks at me and gives me an eye roll, but not before she throws it into park and opens the driver's side door.

I open mine, hop out, and meet her in front of the headlights. She tries her best to get around me, but I snag an arm around her waist and pull her to me, kicking and screaming. I give her no choice but to look me in the eyes.

"Raegan, look at me, please," I try to say without getting upset. "Please, I love you. I've never told anyone about us or you or your grandaddy." And, in that moment, I know I've slipped up, and a tornado is about to break loose. She tries to push back from me, and there is fear in her eyes.

"What do you mean about Grandaddy?" Tears begin to fill her eyes. I have to decide to be upfront about everything or act like I'm clueless. I can't lie to her now that I've messed up.

"Rae, I know he's sick. You don't have to lie to me anymore," I answer as I try to embrace her, but she goes into a full-out storm of emotions just as Cole had predicted.

CHAPTER 29

Raegan

When Emmett slipped up, I was hurt, pissed, and wanted to scream to the top of my lungs. *What gives him the right to know? Cole better not have told him! I'm gonna beat his ass, I swear!*

"Who told you?" I seethe.

He shakes his head. "Tell me!" I say, beating his chest with my fists. "Tell me!" He continues to refuse.

Speaking softly, he replies, "I promised not to tell." I continue to hit him harder until I have no fight left in me. He pulls me so close to his chest I can't move my arms. With my arms feeling like they are in a straightjacket, I give up moving, but I beg one more time. "Pleassseee, tell me, Em. Who told you?" My fear, anger, and hurt are replaced by an overwhelming wave of hopelessness.

"Rae, I love you. I will never leave you, and you can count on me for *anything*. It doesn't matter who told me. It only matters that I can be here for you now." My body gives in, and I crumble in his arms. Without another word, he lifts me from the ground, embraces me in his steady arms, and places me into the passenger side before taking me home.

As Emmett drives down the road, I don't speak. Instead, I stare out the window and replay the events of the night and try to see into the future. The hardest part about the future is the unknown, and right now, I'd give my life to be able to see what our future holds.

Emmett doesn't take me directly back to the farm; he takes me down to the side road by the creek.

"Em, what are you doin'?" I whisper.

"Rae, I'm not taking you home like this. We're gonna figure it out after you tell me what exactly is goin' on," he says with compassion in his voice. I nod in agreement as tears fill my eyes and begin to flow down my face. Emmett puts the truck into park and turns to look at me. Almost as if I'm taken back in time, I remove my seatbelt and crawl into his arms, as a child would do to their parents. In the seat of the truck, I let down my guard completely and all the pent-up emotions from the past couple of months come flooding through. I let Emmett see the real me—the girl who has lost her parents, who is losing the most important person in her life and is uncertain of what her future holds.

He rubs his hands in my hair and continues to try to calm me, and when I can no longer cry, I begin to speak as my body begins to shake.

"Em, I don't know what I'm gonna do. I've lost everyone important to me, and I can't lose him. Not now or ever. I'm so thankful you walked back into my life." I wipe the tears from my face and wait for him to respond.

"Rae, he's a fighter. He doesn't give up easily. He's worked for everything he has, and I know he's gonna give this his best shot. He needs you to live your life. Regardless, you have me, and I'm never leaving."

"How can I live my life? He *is* my life!"

"I understand that, but you remember what Mufasa told Simba, don't ya?" *What the heck? Did he just reference The Lion King?*

"Ummm, I think so, but I don't want to talk about the dang Circle of Life. I want Grandaddy to live forever because that's what he's supposed to do. He's always met everything head-on, lived life to the fullest, and he's gonna outlive me. That's how it's supposed to be. Not like this."

Emmett must know not to push me further. He places his hand on my cheek. "Rae, I know this is tough, and I know you like to be in control, but sometimes life tests us, and this is a test for you, your grandaddy, and the rest of us. Let's make a deal?"

"What kinda deal?" I ask.

"Let's try not to worry about the future. Instead, let's focus on the present. I don't know what's gonna happen, but I do know that as long as we all have each other, it will work out like it should. Who knows? This could work, and he'll be back to his normal self. He's healthy as a dang horse other than *this*."

"You can say it, ya know? Leukemia. I'm not scared of what it is, but I'm petrified of what it will do to him," I state.

"Like I said, let's see how this goes, and Cole and I will be with y'all every step of the way."

I nod in agreement. "Do I have to go home tonight?" I ask him.

"Well, unless I have a death wish, yes, you do. Why?"

"Got any of that shine left? I wanna get drunk and take advantage of you," I say with a small smile. Even though I know that's not how I should handle this situation.

"Raegan Lowery! I'd love to take you up on that offer, but I'm not gonna let you use my body to push your feelings to the side. I will let you get sloppy drunk and take you home, where I can lay you in the bed and make sure you're okay. I will help you forget that way, but I will not let you tarnish what we have between us. I love you too much."

Those words sting, but I know he is speaking from the heart. I will thank him for it in the morning, as long as I'm not hugging a toilet. "Get me the jar." Emmett shakes his head as he goes to get the remainder of the moonshine, but before we make our way to the creek bank, I see the screen light up on his phone. *Wonder who he's texting?*

"Who was that?" I ask him as we sit down.

"Cole. I wanted him to know where we were and to let your grandaddy know you might be late for curfew."

"Are you kiddin' me?" I ask.

"Nope, I didn't want him to worry. Plus, I wanted Cole to know what happened tonight."

"Thanks, I guess. Are you okay? I mean, I know you won the fight, but you're gonna have one heck of a shiner in the morning."

"Yeah, I'll be fine. As long as I have you, there's no need to worry."

I look at the water as I say the next words. "I've just never had anyone besides Grandaddy and Cole care so much about me."

"Rae, from this day forward, you will never have to worry about how I feel about you. I'm never leaving you. I'm your present and your future."

"How do you know that?"

"I know I've never felt what I do for anyone else, and I can't picture my life without you. It's almost like I feel complete."

He's just explained how I feel about him. He's the other

half to my whole, and if I had pushed him away tonight, I would have never recovered. I begin to smile inside, because as another mountain in my life is created, an angel has appeared to guide me through.

Emmett

After the bottle of shine is empty, Raegan and I sit and stare across the water without saying a word. The night sky is clear, and the smell of fresh hay bales permeates the air. Just as I'm about to break the silence, Raegan beats me to it.

"I miss them, ya know," she slurs as she hugs her knees. "People think I don't remember, but I do. Just because I was five doesn't mean I didn't understand. I did. I remember the look on my grandaddy's face, going to the hospital, and the men in suits. That's what I can't shake from my mind. The men in suits. They were so distinct and almost untouchable. That's what scares me the most about Grandaddy being sick. I remember every move they made at the funeral, and I don't want to relive that again. They were like the constant reminder that it was *real*. I mean, I don't want Grandaddy to suffer, and I know he's lived a good life, but I can't face the men in suits. For me, that will make it *real*."

I turn to look at her as tears begin to stream down her face as well as mine. In this moment, I feel her pain. I want nothing more than to take it away from her mind, body, and soul and insert it into mine.

"Rae, I still remember. The men in suits, that is, but what I remember the most is the look on your face when you were at the front of the church. You stood down there with a smile on your face, but when I looked you in the eyes, I saw how sad you were. It's never left me, and as a child, I felt your fear. On that day, I knew I had to do something to make you feel better. That's why I brought the bunny. I knew you loved Thumper. I thought it might make you smile."

She turns to look at me while wiping her tears, and I have no idea what she is about to say. "Em, you don't understand. When my world came crashing down, I didn't know what to do. Grandaddy's house had always been a fun place to visit, but on the way home from the funeral I realized it was no longer a fun place to visit. It was now my home. Em, I can still remember wanting my mama to tuck me in that night and having to remind myself that she couldn't." She takes a minute to collect her thoughts and then begins to speak again.

"Then, you showed up with that stuffed bunny. It was almost as if my mama sent you to me. The day you brought it, it was like I found a little bit of hope in this world. I realized people do love me, and that life would get better. You know what's funny about all of this?" she says as she looks for an answer.

"What?" I reply.

"When things get hard and I want to give up, I hold on to that bunny and remember the moment you gave it to me. It's almost as if I was trying to hold on to you even when you weren't here. Like it was my guardian when you weren't around. Does that sound crazy?"

Taking my arm and wrapping it around her shoulder, I pull her close. "No, Rae, it doesn't sound crazy, but I never knew it meant that much to you."

"Em, your sweet gesture gave me hope, just like you being here with me now does. I'm so glad you know."

I feel a little bit better, knowing she is okay with me finding out about her grandaddy. I knew I couldn't lie to her anymore, and I didn't care if she pushed me away, because I wasn't walking out of her life, ever.

As Raegan begins to get quiet, I hold her until she falls asleep in my arms, and then place her in the truck to take her home. Making my way up the steps, I'm met by Mr. Lowery. He shakes his head and tells me once I take her to her room to come and sit a few minutes with him. Something about this conversation tells me that things are about to change for sure.

Making my way back downstairs, I hear Mr. Lowery in the kitchen. I enter and see him pouring two classes of sweet tea. As he approaches me, he hands me a glass of tea and a bag of frozen peas.

"Have a seat, Emmett. I'm not sure what happened tonight, but you're gonna need to get something on that eye of yours before it swells anymore." I don't answer, instead I place the frozen contents on my eye.

"Emmett, things have been rough around here for a while. I feel awful for making Sunshine feel like she has to keep it from everyone, but I was hoping that this would be a quick fix. Undoubtedly, it's not going to be. I'm not exactly sure how long these treatments are actually going to work. I'm tired of her always worrying about me, and I want this to be between us and Cole. I want to watch her *live*. Can you help me do that?

In this moment, I know his secret is more than Raegan ever imagined. "Yes, sir. I'll do whatever you need me to do, and I promise to *always* be there for her."

CHAPTER 30

Raegan

With the sound of the alarm, my head begins to throb in rhythm. *I think I'm dying. Why do I feel like I've been run over twice? Oh, no! Hurry! Hurry!* I make it to the bathroom in the nick of time. As the contents spew from my stomach, I recall the events in the wee hours of the morning. *I think I'm gonna die!* There is a knock at the door, interrupting me.

"Sunshine, are you okay?" Grandaddy asks as he stays on the other side of the door.

"I will be. Might be slow moving, though," I mumble.

"Okay, meet me at the kitchen table."

"Yes, sir," I say as I meet the porcelain throne, yet again. When I have nothing left to expel, I splash water onto my face, change clothes, pop a few pain relievers, and make my way to the kitchen.

"Rough mornin'?" he questions.

"More like the stupidity won last night. Why did I think that was a good idea?"

"Come here. Have a seat." I do as he asks while he pours me a cup of coffee and makes me a breakfast plate. *Oh gosh! I don't know if I can eat this.* "Raegan, I don't agree with how you chose to handle this situation, but I'm thankful Emmett respects me enough to call me."

"Did he..." I start to say, but I am interrupted by Grandaddy.

"Sunshine, you have yourself a man of his word. He brought you home, knocked on my door, made sure you were okay, and then he sat at this table with me and explained what happened last night. Like I said, I don't agree with it one bit, but we all have to escape reality from time to time. For that, I'll give you a pass this go round, but not again. Never drown your feelings with the liquid courage within a glass jar. It might feel good at the time, but it always comes back to bite you in the morning. I love you, and I will not let you make that your escape. It will only hurt you in the end."

Taking a few bites, I begin to feel somewhat alive, and I assure Grandaddy that I will not do that again.

"You better hurry up, Sunshine. We gotta be at church in an hour." *Crap! I didn't even think about that.*

The entire time I'm listening to the preacher, I can hear my stomach churning as if it's trying to tell the world what I chose to do last night. *Enough already!* At exactly noon, we walk out the wooden doors, and Emmett greets me.

"Rae, 'bout last night."

I take his hand in mine, replying, "Thank you." Those are the only words that need to be spoken. He kisses my cheek, and Grandaddy informs me that he is going out to eat with Joe. He then proceeds to ask Emmett if he minds taking me out for lunch and back home this afternoon. Of course, he doesn't, and I can't help but wonder what Grandaddy is really up to.

After Emmett and I eat lunch, we hang out at my house. Since I no longer feel hungover, we take a ride over the farm and return to the spot where I spilled my entire bottled-up feelings from the past twelve years last night. He stops, and I glance over my shoulder at him.

"Whatcha thinkin', Rae?" he questions.

"I'm thinking how did I get so lucky," I say as I turn to face him.

"Rae, it's not luck. It's how our story was bound to play out. I'm almost certain three individuals are looking down on us and cheering us on." The thought of my mawmaw and parents smiling down on me makes me feel alive.

"I guess you're right. Sometimes I hope they turn their heads and don't watch, though." Emmett has a stunned look on his face. "Ya know, there are some things that parents don't need to watch their children do." As he catches on, I burst out laughing. He slides his arms around my waist and pulls me toward him.

"Yeah, I hope you're right."

"Wanna make them turn their head?" I ask with a wink.

Emmett

Dang, that girl is going to be the death of me, but if I die loving her, I'd be happy with that. Then, the reality of my words set in. *Death.* I never want to leave her, and tomorrow, her world is going to change, either for the better or for the worse. Which one, we don't know, but I know regardless of Mr. Lowery's outcome, I'm not going anywhere.

After we make our way back to the house, I tell her I'll go with them to the hospital in the morning. Of course, she refuses and says one of us needs to go to school. All of that has to do with appearances. If we are both absent, people will talk, and that's what her grandaddy doesn't want. She also informs me that she is going tomorrow to really get a feel for things. She doesn't know if Cole and her grandaddy are trying to hide things from her.

***

When my alarm goes off, I make sure I hurry to get ready, so I can talk to Cole before I leave for school. After I knock on his door, he tells me to come inside.

"What's up, Em?" he asks.

"I was just wondering if you would keep an eye on my girl today."

"Of course, I will. How 'bout you not lay Jace out at school today?"

"I take it you heard about it."

"Word travels fast in a small town," he replies, and I laugh. He promises to be there for Mr. Lowery and Raegan. I can't express how thankful I am for him. "Now, get out of here before you're tardy."

"I'm goin'," I say as I make my way downstairs, grab a Pop Tart, and walk to my truck.

As I pull into the parking lot at school, I'm greeted by none other than Jace. *Happy Freakin' Monday!*

"Jace," I say as I shut my door. He doesn't say anything; he just stands there. "Are you gonna move or what?"

"Are you gonna make me?" he smarts back.

"No, I don't want any trouble."

"Who said anything 'bout trouble? I just want to finish what we started."

"Jace, there's nothing to finish, but I am curious, though. What made you say that to Raegan? You know she's not like that."

Jace smirks as he takes a step forward. "See, that's where you're wrong. I just made that up, but the way you jumped on me proved me right. Just wanted to clear this up for ya. *You let the world know your business. I just left the bait.*" *What do I say to that? Nothing. I say nothing.* I take a step to the left of Jace then stop. As I'm trying to talk myself out of doing something stupid yet again, Jace starts to laugh, and that pisses me off. Catching him off guard, I turn back to my right, grab him by his shirt, and push him backwards until he is pressed against my truck.

"You listen to me, Jace. You didn't prove anything except how much of a jerk you really are. If you think this will make Raegan push me away, you are wrong. Raegan is *mine*, not *yours*. Next time you decide to pull some crap like this, I'm going to make sure you never see the light of day. You got me?" I say as I push him hard against the truck one more time before turning to leave.

CHAPTER 31

Raegan

After feeding all the farm animals, I go inside to get ready for a day I never wanted to happen, but it's reality. Grandaddy is sick, and this is the only way for him to survive. Once I'm showered and dressed for the day, I eat breakfast, and Grandaddy and I carry on our normal morning conversation as we wait for Cole.

As I finish washing the dishes, Cole walks inside the house. He looks so well put together, but when I look at him, I can sense he's as scared as the rest of us.

"Mornin'. Y'all save me anything?" he asks.

"Yeah, your plate is on the stove," I reply.

"Awesome," he says, grabbing his plate and coffee and taking a seat at the table. "How are you feelin', Uncle Dover?" he asks mid-bite.

"Healthy as a horse for now. Hurry up, or we're gonna be late," Grandaddy states.

Once Cole finishes his breakfast, we head out the door. Cole drives his truck, and before we know it, we are at Cleveland Hematology and Oncology.

I try to push my fears out of my head as we make our way inside the building. This isn't going to be the hard part. I have a feeling the next few days are what is going to be tough.

As Grandaddy is taken back, Cole and I sit in the waiting room until he gets settled, and then we are allowed inside the room with him.

"Rae, are you hangin' in there?" Cole asks.

"Yeah, I guess. How was Em this morning?" *Because I would rather talk about Em than this.*

"Worried about you. I told him not to clobber Jace today, and everything would be great." He laughs.

"Ohmygosh! Cole, it was crazy! One minute everything was okay, and the next, all crap broke loose. I don't know what I would have done if it got bad." Before we can finish our conversation, the nurse calls us back. I look toward Cole, and he takes my hand in his and squeezes it.

As we walk through the door to the large room full of recliners, all I see is white. Everything is bright, sterile, and white. Then, I notice all the people in the chairs. Each of them is covered with a blanket, and the majority of them look feeble. I spot Grandaddy on the right side, and my heart shatters as I see him surrounded by cords and monitors. He smiles at us as we approach.

"Wipe that look off your face, Sunshine. If you are gonna mope, I'm sendin' ya to school. You got it?" he says with a little attitude.

"Yes, sir." I smile because at least he doesn't have one of those blankets. "How are ya?"

"Okay, now that they've quit stickin' me. I guess I shoulda got that port-a-cath thingy. Oh well, I'll just have new battle wounds."

"Anything we can do, Uncle Dover?" Cole asks.

"Yep, get me that fishing magazine outta your truck. I'm gonna be here about two hours they said. Y'all might want to find something to pass the time."

That's easy for me. I pull out my kindle and begin to read Jillian Dodd's newest release.

"Whatcha readin'?" Cole asks.

"*Adore Me.*"

"Is that the one about Moon Boy or somethin'?" Cole questions.

"Yup. Still don't know, but I'm hoping it's Aiden or Brooklyn. Who knows?!" I say.

"I don't get you girls and your books," he says as he shakes his head.

"Me either," Grandaddy chimes in.

We spend the next two hours reading, talking, helping Grandaddy stay comfortable, and making the nurse laugh. I believe she's gonna remember us, for sure. Once Grandaddy is finished, they check his vitals, and we make our way to the truck. Grandaddy begins to walk slower than normal. I don't say a word; I just put my arm in his for support.

"I love you, Sunshine," he says.

"I love you more, Grandaddy."

Once we arrive back at the farm, I help Grandaddy get comfortable before going to school. Cole is going to keep an eye on him until I get home today. *Thank goodness, cheerleading is over for now.*

"Are you sure you're okay?" I question before leaving.

"Yes, Raegan, I'm fine. Now, get on to school before I drag you there myself."

"I gotcha. I'll be home after school. Call me if I need to pick up anything on the way." He nods, and I kiss the top of his bald head before telling Cole to call me if anything happens. I leave and put the truck in the wind.

I arrive halfway through third block, and have totally missed lunch. *Dang, I'm gonna be starving by three o'clock.* Pushing it to the side, I pull my notebook and pencil from my bag and take notes like a mad woman.

As the bell rings to end the day, I exit class to head to my locker, but come face-to-face with Jace instead.

"Hey, Jace, how are ya?" I decide to be a Southern Belle and play nice.

"I'm good. Have you seen Emmett today?" he prods.

"No, I came in late today. What's it matter to you anyway?" I ask.

"Ask your boyfriend," he says and walks away. That was totally weird, and for some reason I feel as if things have gone from bad to worse.

Rounding the corner, I see Emmett waiting on me at my locker, and a smile develops across my face.

"Hey, Em," I say as I wrap my arms around him in a tight squeeze. "Gosh, I missed you."

"I missed you, too," he says, but I can tell his mind is elsewhere.

"He's doin' okay," I say into his ear.

"Good. Rae, I need to talk to you." *Oh gosh. I feel my stomach begin on a rollercoaster ride.*

"Sure. Is everything okay? I mean, I ran into Jace a few minutes ago and he said to ask you what was wrong with him. Why would he do that?"

He doesn't reply. *Something's not right. What is he not telling me? Is he gonna break up with me. What have I done?* Then, my mind stops spinning out of control as my eyes land on Jace across the hallway. *That POS! He's up to something.* I get my nerves under control as we make our way to my truck.

"Hey, why don't you meet me at the creek? I don't want an audience," I say. Emmett looks at me like he's caught off guard by my reaction. "Plus, I gotta get home to Grandaddy."

He nods, and once he closes my truck door, he makes his way to his truck and follows me to the creek. As I wait for him, I send Cole a quick text before getting out.

"So, what's up?" I question with my arms crossed.

"Rae, I'm to blame for what happened Saturday night."

Confusion engulfs my body. "But, you said you didn't tell anyone?" I question as fear rises in my throat.

"I didn't, but Jace did that on purpose. He wanted to know. He baited me, and I fell for it. Hook, line, and sinker."

"I'm no blonde, but I think I might need you to explain," I say as calmly as possible.

Jace didn't know anything about us, but I guess he assumed. Anyway, when he made that comment about you, he knew by my reaction it was true. So, he didn't tell the world. I did without even knowing," he says as he waits for my response.

I close my eyes and replay what he has just told me. Everyone knows our business because Jace baited Emmett. He was just trying to protect me, but if I hadn't let him in, there would be nothing to tell. *Oh gosh, I'm gonna be sick.* I lose everything I had for breakfast.

"Rae, are you okay?" Emmett asks as he hurries to my side.

"I'm fine," I say as I take a step away from him. As my reality smacks me in the face, I become angry. Not really at Emmett, but just at the world in general. "I'm sorry, Em, but I just can't do this today." I walk toward my truck and leave him dumbfounded.

"Rae, wait!" he yells as he runs to catch me. "Please,

don't leave me."

I turn abruptly to him. "I never said I was leaving. I said I *'can't* do this." I point to us. "Not today. I've been on a rollercoaster ride of emotions since Saturday night, and if this mess between you and Jace continues, we are done. Grandaddy needs me right now and I won't watch you two fight over me."

"You can't, Rae. I love you."

"I love you, too, Em. That's why I have to go. I can't put you through this mess. I love you too much."

Emmett tries to keep me from getting into my truck. He eventually realizes my mind is made up. It's not that I don't want to be with him, because I do. I just can't right now. I need to focus on Grandaddy.

Emmett

As Raegan tells me she can't be with me anymore, I feel the air leave my lungs, and I don't know if I am going to survive. That girl is everything to me. I knew telling her was a risk, but I had to tell her. She couldn't hear it from Jace, and I knew sooner or later that was going to happen.

As she pulls away in her truck, I watch because I can't move. The only thing that gives me hope is her telling me she can't do this *right now,* and right now *isn't* forever. From this point forward, I'll give her space with her grandaddy, but when the time comes, I'll be there like I never left.

CHAPTER 32

Raegan

I hightail it back to the farm. Not only has Jace managed to ruin my relationship with Emmett, but he also helped me realize what I need to truly focus on right now.

As I park the truck, Cole meets me. "Care to explain what the heck just happened between you and Emmett?"

"Nothing," I say as I try to walk past him, but he puts a stop to it quickly.

"'Nothing,' my ass. That boy loves you, and he only reacted that way because he didn't want someone talking 'bout you like that. I know life sucks right now, but don't go through it alone. He wants to be here for you, me, *and* Uncle Dover."

"I just told him I couldn't do this right now. I didn't mean forever. Just. Right. Now. Cole, Grandaddy needs me more."

"I understand, but you broke him." Hearing Cole say those words makes my heart crack, but my mind is made up. It isn't about Emmett, Cole, or my feelings. It is about helping Grandaddy survive.

"Whatever, Rae. I just hope he's still around when you

come to your senses. This is the stupidest thing you've ever done."

"Ughhhhhh!" I huff as I push into him and make my way toward the house.

As I clomp up the steps, I swing open the screen door with all my might. Grandaddy turns to look at me from his recliner.

"What's wrong with you?" he asks.

"Nothing, except I'm done with Emmett for now."

"What'd you do that for?" he banters back.

"Don't worry about it. I just want it to be you and me for now."

"Sunshine—"

I cut him off. "No. This is it, end of discussion," I say, and he doesn't respond because he knows I'm just like him, and when my mind is made up, there's no changing it.

Over the next week, Emmett continues to blow up my phone, but I ignore him. He tries to talk to me at lunch, but I sit at the opposite end of the table beside Jordyn. She doesn't understand what's going on, but she doesn't question. Other than the whispers from people about Emmett and me breaking up, everything continues like usual. No one has a clue about Grandaddy. He's doing okay, and he only has one more treatment because his numbers are doing so well. I begin to feel some hope in my life, and I want to talk to Emmett about it, but I won't do that yet. I need to make sure everything is back to normal. *I think I need to talk to Cole.* I pull out my phone and text him to hang around until I get home today.

Emmett

The moment I lay my eyes on her after school, I know

her life is about to change. I'm thankful to have Cole in my life. When Raegan pushed me away, Cole pulled me in closer. He knew how I felt as well as her. He kept me informed through all the treatments, visits, and her smiles and tears. I'll never be able to repay him for that. When he called me saying Mr. Lowery was cancer-free, I had to see the truth in her eyes before she let the calm waters predict our future.

As she approaches, I can see her hesitation. I'm not going to talk to her, but when her eyes meet mine, I stare into her soul like I did months ago. She still loves me, and after today, I pray she'll let me back into her life, but there would be one difference. If life gets tough ever again, I am not leaving, no matter how hard she pushes me away. I love her too dang much.

Raegan

As I walk to my truck after school, I notice Emmett is parked beside me. *Oh gosh. Oh gosh. I'm not ready for this.* I smile as I pass him and make my way to the driver's side. He smiles back, but doesn't approach me. In that moment, my heart cries because I think he might be moving on, and if I've lost him, it's no one's fault but my own. As I go to put the truck in drive, I notice an envelope on the console. Putting the truck back in park, I open it and smile as I read the words from Em.

When I think of Raegan Lowery, I see sunshine. I see a girl who's unstoppable, but hides her feelings from the world. Raegan Lowery isn't perfect, but it's her imperfections that make her perfect for me. She's what my perfect girl is designed to be. She's the girl that makes me feel alive, and she's the reason I want to live. I love her, and I know that she loves me too.

R-eal as they come

E-ndures and pushes forward

A-ttached to the ones she loves

G-uards her heart

A-chieves anything she puts her mind to

N-ow has my heart

As I stare at the words Emmett has written, my heart warms, and I know that it's time to let him back into my life. I put the truck into drive and hurry to meet Cole.

"Hey, Cole," I say as I get out of the truck, but he's sprinting toward me. He meets me with a huge hug. "Are you okay?" I ask.

"You bet! You need to get in there." I don't know whether to be happy or scared.

"Okay, but I need to talk to you." He follows me inside, and I see Grandaddy shelling pecans as he watches a basketball game on TV.

"Hey, Grandaddy," I say as I walk to him. A big grin covers his face. "What's that grin for?"

"Oh, ya know, Dr. Charles called with my blood work, and we're good. No need to do that last one." *Did I just hear that right?* "You heard me right, Sunshine. I'm cancer-free."

Tears begin to pour down my face from pure joy. I turn to look at Cole, and he's crying, too. *We did it! We got through this. No one knew. He's gonna be okay.*

"Now, quit the crying. I hope to be back to full-time work in the next week. I plan on driving into town tomorrow and going out to dinner with my buddies. They were startin' to get suspicious."

"Sounds good. Hey, Cole, I think I need to take a ride. Do you wanna go with me?" I ask.

"Sure. I bet I can beat ya to the fence post."

"Yeah, right," I say mid-run toward the door. Cole and I

race to the fence line, and when we reach it, I'm completely shocked when I see Emmett standing against it. I turn to look at Cole, and he shrugs his shoulders.

"I figured it was time to get back to living, Rae. Don't be mad at me," Cole says and then turns back toward the house.

I turn off the ignition and slowly make my way to him. "How'd you know I'd be here?"

"There are some things between Cole and me that you will never understand. He's not my blood brother, but he is my brother. He's kept me informed, told me about everything. I knew today when you walked to your truck that your life was about to change for the better. I couldn't miss it, and it's good to know we know you well enough to know when things are at either extreme—good or bad—you take them out on this field. I'm just glad Cole clued me in," he says as he walks toward me.

When we are a foot apart, he stops. "Rae, I know why you pushed me away. It's made my life unbearable for the past couple of months, but knowing Cole was there for you helped. I love you with my entire heart, and I can't wait to have you back in my life."

"What makes you think I'm ready?" I ask as I look into his eyes.

"The fact you didn't follow Cole back gave me a little reassurance, but the way your eyes fell on mine today warmed my heart. I knew you were ready."

"Em, I'm so sorry I pushed you away, but that's what I felt I needed to do. I've never stopped loving you, and now I know you never stopped either." I say as I take a step toward him and place my hands upon his firm chest.

"Rae, I'll love you as long as I'm alive," he declares as he places his hand behind my neck, and my lips meet his like they never left.

CHAPTER 33

Raegan

When I walk back into the house, Grandaddy looks over his shoulder at me. "'Bout time," he says before turning back to the TV. I just shake my head and think about all the men that love me.

Over the next two months, life returns to normal. Grandaddy is back to his full capacity on the farm, Cole and Tammy are spending a lot of time together, and Emmett and I...well, we are together every chance we get. I love him more and more each day. Jace has finally gotten over himself and doesn't get in our business anymore.

As March approaches, we begin to prepare for the summer crops, and I can't wait to go to the Braves game with Grandaddy, Cole, Tammy, and Emmett.

"Hey, Grandaddy, I got those tickets ordered," I say as I come downstairs to cook supper.

"Allll righhht!" he says. *I could listen to him say that over and over.*

We eat supper, watch the ACC Tournament, and then retire for the night. Glancing at my calendar, I realize it's been six months since Grandaddy got the news, and I know he has to go back for a check-up sometime soon. *I'll have to ask him about that in the morning.* I drift off and wake up to live my life to the fullest on the farm and at school.

At breakfast, I ask Grandaddy about his appointment. "Oh, it was last week. It was fine. Go back in six more months."

"Why didn't you tell me? I'd have gone with you."

"I know, but I'm fine. You need to be at school. Education is what is important."

"I know. I know," I say as I finish eating and leave for school.

Emmett meets me in the parking lot, and to be honest, I couldn't wait to lay my eyes on him. I swear, it's a good thing we have school to distract us.

"Mornin', Beautiful," he says as he greets me with a kiss.

"Mornin'."

"You sure are chipper this morning."

"Grandaddy got great news. Everything is still good. Oh! And, I got the Braves tickets for this summer." Emmett begins the tomahawk chop and sings the chant. I just shake my head.

I meet Jordyn in the hall, and she looks like a wreck. "What's wrong?" I ask.

"It's just Ridge. He's being an ass."

"What did he do?" I inquire sincerely.

"He told me that my butt looks big in these jeans. Can you believe that?" *Ohmygosh! Seriously!*

"J, are you kiddin' me?! I thought he broke up with you or somethin'. You got yourself an honest one. You knew that when you started dating him."

She shakes her head. "I swear, sometimes I wish he'd just not tell the truth for once." We both laugh as we walk to class.

As we sit at lunch, Emmett looks at me for guidance on the situation earlier. "We're all good," I whisper as we sit down.

"Good," he says as he kisses my cheek quickly.

"Hey, I have an idea," Jordyn says.

"Oh, brother," I say with an eye roll and a laugh.

"Let's go to my mountain house this weekend. Ya know, get away from here. You in, Rae?" she suggests, as she looks in my direction.

"Let me check with Grandaddy, but I think we should be good. Who's all game?" As I look around, Jordyn, Ridge, Emmett, and I are all in.

"Make sure you keep it quiet. I mean, Cole and what's her name can come, but I don't want those meatheads to think it's an open invitation."

"Gotcha."

As the bell rings for class, Emmett pulls me back from the crowd and lightly guides me under the stairs before attacking my lips. I kiss him back, but not for long, because Mr. Wall catches us and tells us to quit locking lips before he has to call my grandaddy. I giggle as Emmett walks me to class and then promises to meet me after school.

After school, he's waiting on me as usual. "Hey, Em," I say as I greet him with a kiss. "So, you think your mama's gonna let you go?" I ask.

"Yeah, especially if Cole goes. You have more to worry about than me."

"Nah, as long as Cole is going, he'll let me."

"Ya know, something's not right about that. He's my brother, not yours." He laughs.

"But, if you hurt me, he'll beat your ass." I smirk.

"Got me there," he says as he kisses me goodbye, and I

make my way home.

As I approach the farm, I see Cole working in the lower field. *I gotta go see if he's in for the weekend.* I put away my backpack and grab a can of Sun Drop for both Cole and me as I make my way out there.

"Thanks, Rae," he says. "What's up?"

"Ah, ya know, hoping to go to J's mountain house this weekend. You wanna go?"

"You're totally using me, aren't ya?" He smirks.

"You bet. So, are you in or what? Tammy can come, too," I state with my hand on my hips.

"Yeah, as long as Uncle Dover is game. I mean, it's not like he's stupid or anything." I let my mouth fall open and then push his shoulder. "I'm just speakin' the truth."

"Whatever," I say as I make my way inside the house to ask Grandaddy.

Once inside, I smell supper underway. "Grandaddy!" I yell as I come through the door.

"I'm in the kitchen!" he hollers back.

As I enter the kitchen, I see him in his apron standing over a pot of pintos, tasting them. "Just makin' sure they're good enough to eat," he says. "How was your day?"

"Great, actually. Do we have any plans this weekend?' He shakes his head no. "Can I go to Jordyn's mountain house?"

He pauses for a moment. "Who's goin'?" *Oh crap! He's on to my game already.*

"Jordyn, Ridge, Cole, Tammy, Em, and me." He stares right at me.

He takes the spoon still in his hand and shakes it at me. "Sunshine, did you go to the doctor?"

"Yeah, what made you ask that six months down the road?"

"Heck, a lot of stuff went on, and it kinda slipped my mind. Plus, when y'all broke up, I didn't have much to worry about. Now, I do," he says as he begins to make a cake of cornbread. I walk to the hall closet, grab my apron, and begin to help him.

"So, can I go?" I ask as I grab the buttermilk from the fridge.

He stops and turns to me. "Rae, I think you need to get away. Things have been crazy for the past six months, but I want you to be smart. I also know you will find a way to get your way. You always have." *Well, he's never said I get my way before. That's odd.* "You said Cole was goin'?"

"Yes, sir," I reply as I pour the buttermilk.

"That's why you were butterin' him up with that Sun Drop earlier, huh?"

"*Maybe.*"

"What am I going to do with you?" he asks. "Fine, but please, don't do anything stupid."

"Grandaddy, I can't believe you'd say that."

"Hey, I was young once."

"Oh, I know, and you were like the stud of your graduating class."

"I wasn't the stud. I was voted best-looking, thank ya very much." We both laugh.

"Do you think they are looking down on us?" I ask him as I stir the cornbread mixture.

"Sunshine, I have no doubt. We wouldn't have made it this far without them cheering for us." We both smile as I wipe a single tear from my eye.

"Um, um, um…this is gonna be good," he says as we place the cornbread into the oven and watch the evening news until time to eat.

Emmett

I. Cannot. Wait. A weekend away with Raegan is just what I need. Now, if Mom will let me go. Thank goodness for Cole.

Mom is folding laundry when I get home from school. I go in and help her, and she stops mid-fold.

"What's going on, Em?" she asks with her hand on her hips.

"I just wanted to know if it was okay if I went to the mountains this weekend with Cole, Tammy, Jordyn, Ridge, and Rae."

"Em, are you sure that is a good idea?"

"Yeah, it'll be fine!" I hear Cole holler as he enters the house. *Cole to the rescue.* "First, we gotta see if Uncle Dover lets *her* go." He laughs.

"You're right, Cole. If Dover will let her go, I guess I should trust you enough. Just don't get that girl pregnant for cryin' out loud." Cole bursts out laughing as he leaves the room.

"Um, Mom. Are you okay?" I question with caution.

"Lord, yes, I'm fine, but I know what it's like to be young and dumb. Please, be smarter than your father and me." She doesn't have to explain anymore because I know I was a mishap when they were seniors in high school. Needless to say, I can see why she worries.

"Mom, no need to worry. I wouldn't put you or Mr. Lowery through that, but I do think Raegan needs to get away. She's had a lot going on over the past few months."

"Yes, I know *they* have, Em. I know they like their secrets, but Dover always keeps George and Cole in the loop.

As you know, George and I don't have secrets." *My mom knew the entire time? No wonder she didn't question when we broke up. She already knew why.*

"Why didn't you tell me?" I ask.

"Because it wasn't my place to tell." It almost feels like déjà vu. "Now, get outta here, unless you really want to fold clothes."

"Yes, ma'am," I say as I hug her on my way out of the room.

As I pass Cole's room, he hollers for me to come in. "So, she said okay?"

"Yup, I take it Rae got to you right after school. You think he'll let her go?"

"He probably will give her crap for it, but yeah, she always gets her way."

"Cole, thanks for everything."

"No problem. Do you have a minute?" Cole questions.

"I guess. What's up?" I ask as I take a seat in the chair.

Cole is rubbing the back of his neck, and right now, I'm not sure what he's about to say.

"Um, I don't know if I should tell you this or not, but I don't think Uncle Dover's out of the woods." My heart stops. I know that Cole and I both share Mr. Lowery's secret.

"I know, Cole." He looks completely shocked. "He told me when he decided not to take the last treatment. What do you think Rae's gonna do when she finds out we knew the entire time?"

"I think she's going to be royally ticked off, and that's an understatement." Cole and I devise a plan to talk with Mr. Lowery and her once we get back from our fun weekend. These secrets are over, and it's time we do this together.

Trying to get out of our deep conversation, Cole brings

things back to reality. "I better make sure Tammy is in. I sure don't want to be the fifth wheel," he says as he takes out his phone to call her, and I close the door as I head to my room.

CHAPTER 34

Raegan

Friday afternoon feels like it will never get here, but eventually, it does. We all hurry home from school and finish packing. I help Grandaddy around the farm with a few things, and we are on the road by five.

The house is a little over an hour and a half away from Pleasant Hill. It's perfect for a weekend getaway. As the house comes into view, I get butterflies. I can remember coming here with Jordyn when we were kids during every season. It was a perfect escape from the farm life, but yet, I was still enjoying nature at its best. Emmett looks my way and squeezes my hand.

"Why are you cheesing over there?" Emmett inquires.

"Just thinkin' about when J and I came here when we were younger. We used to have the best time here."

"I bet." As Cole puts the truck into park, I throw open the door and take off running. I know the game, and Jordyn does as well, because she's neck and neck with me as we make our way to the door. As she tries to slide me out of the way to get to the lock, I tell her that's not fair. When the knob is turned, I push her out of the way and laugh as I hurry to the lookout.

"Rae! I'm callin' it!" she yells as I hear her trying to catch up.

"No, first one there gets it," I say as I find the ladder and hustle to the top. As I look out onto the woods around us, I'm taken back in time to when Jordyn and I fought to see who got the view first when we arrived. Needless to say, I won most of the time. She always was in a pair of heels, even as a kid.

Lying on my back, I look around to see this beautiful world in which we live. Even without the leaves on the trees, it's breathtaking. I'm quickly brought out of my euphoria.

"Girl, you are always beating me!" Jordyn says out of breath.

"Leave the heels at home, *Diva*, and you might stand a chance." I laugh as the rest of the gang greets us.

"Y'all care to explain that craziness?" Cole asks. Of course, he's acting like the adult because he is one.

"Come on up and find out," I say. They all crawl up into the space while we sit with our legs crossed. Jordyn and I watch as they feel what we have felt over and over through the years.

"This is amazing," Tammy says. "It's like you are in your own perfect bubble looking out onto this beautiful world."

"Yes, it is," I chime in.

"So, why did y'all take off running like crazy people?" Cole asks.

Jordyn smiles at me, and I let her take it from here. "See, when we were kids, this was our favorite spot. Who am I kidding? It still is, but we always raced to see who would get to see it first."

Emmett raises his hand like he's in class. "Yes, Em," I say with a cackle. "You know you don't have to raise your hand, right?"

"Look, after that, I'm not sure what y'all are gonna do

next. But, I have one question. Please, tell me you didn't tackle the adults to get here first?"

"No! We'd let my daddy get the door open, and then we'd jump from the car. He knew the game, and he got out of our way real quick."

"Yeah, except that time your mama had him come back out to help her get the groceries. He got caught in the J and Rae storm."

Jordyn and I laugh like little kids, but stop abruptly when we realize everyone else doesn't find it as funny. "I guess you had to have been there," I say with a shrug. They all nod in agreement before making their way back down the ladder.

When Emmett starts to move, I grab his arm and tell him to hold on. Then, I hear Jordyn yell at us, "No fooling around up there!"

"Aw, hush!" I yell back at her. I pat the spot next to me, and he slides beside me. I lie back with my arm behind my head, and he does the same. We don't say a word. I want him to experience this with me—peace inside and outside of my soul.

Emmett

As I lie here with Raegan, my heart feels like it is beating out of my chest. My mom always told me when you find the one to never let her go, and in this moment, with God's beautiful Earth surrounding me, I *know* she's the one. I don't interrupt the perfect stillness between us; instead, I wait for her to tell me what to do next. When she doesn't say anything, I find her hand and guide my fingers between hers.

"Em, can we stay here forever?"

"I'd love that, but staying hidden from others isn't what

this world is about. It's about letting your light shine for the world to see. You are a light worth shining, and I'm not letting you hide in this perfect bubble."

She rolls to her side. "Do you always know the perfect things to say to me?"

"No, it's just what I feel in my heart." And, that's the truth in a nutshell.

CHAPTER 35

Raegan

"Hey, Lovebirds! Y'all comin' down? We gotta case of beer and s'mores to make!" I shake my head as we sit up.

"We're comin'!" I yell back, and then we make our way downstairs.

Our night is filled with fun by the campfire with country music blaring, ooey gooey goodness on our hands from the s'mores, and reminiscing over the year. When Cole, Emmett, or I talk, we never mention Grandaddy's cancer. It's in the past and will stay there.

As everyone begins to turn in for the night, Emmett and I remain by the fire. He holds me tightly. We don't talk, but we enjoy just being together. When the flames begin to diminish, we make our way toward the house and to bed.

As the sun rises, I wake to the sound of light snoring, and I realize I'm not at home but in Emmett's arms. *Gosh, I could wake up like this every day.* When I try to move from him, he squeezes me to his body.

"I'm not lettin' you go," he says.

"Well, you better or I'm gonna pee on ya!" I state bluntly.

"Oh, well," he says as he begins to tickle me.

"Stop, Em! Pleaseeeee. Oh gosh! Please!" I say, and when he realizes I'm not joking, he lets me go, and I sprint to the restroom. As I walk back toward him, I shake my head. "That wasn't funny."

"I thought it was hilarious. Oh, and your phone rang." He tosses it to me, and I see I have a missed call from Grandaddy. I hurry to call him back.

"Morning, Grandaddy," I say when he picks up. He lets me know he's doing great, and the farm is perfect. He then proceeds to tell me to behave myself but to have fun. We end the call after he tells me he loves me, and he expects me to be home by mid-afternoon Sunday.

"Is everything okay?" Emmett questions when I hang up.

"Yeah, he sounded great, actually, better than great," I say as I crawl back into his arms, and we doze off for another hour.

When the sun begins to burn through the window, we decide to quit wasting the day and hit the slopes. We all load up and make our way to Sugar Mountain. I'm not much of a skier, but I'm worth a good laugh, that's for sure.

By the time lunch rolls around, I'm no longer on the slope. I'm sitting in a rocking chair with hot chocolate, watching as everyone flies down the mountain. As the sun begins to hide behind the mountain, everyone decides to come in and join me.

"You've been here *all* afternoon?" Emmett asks.

"Yup, there's nothing like a roaring fire and hot chocolate to make it through the afternoon." He smiles and bends down to the rocking chair to meet my lips. "Y'all ready to go?"

"Yeah, Cole's gone to get the truck." We make our way to meet Cole and the rest of the gang. We stop and pick up something to grill for supper and then head back to the house.

We sit outside by the fire, waiting for Ridge to grill the steaks as the music bleeds through the speakers on the patio. This is absolutely perfect. As if Emmett is reading my mind, he walks up behind me and pulls me close. He whispers into my ear, "I love you."

I turn to face him, "I love you, too."

After supper, we gather around the fire for more s'mores and a small round of Truth or Dare. Needless to say, by the end of the night, I've learned more about these five than I've ever wanted to know. I'm definitely not going to look at Cole ever the same again.

When the sun rises, I snuggle closer to Emmett, because who knows when we will ever be able to do this again. Around eleven o'clock, we finally make our way out of the sheets and downstairs. Everyone is lounging on the front porch, laughing, and having a great time before heading home.

After we eat a bite of breakfast, we get ready and then pack to head home. As I fold my clothes into my bag, I glance up to see Emmett staring at me.

"See somethin' you like?" I tease.

"Of course, but you know tomorrow is gonna be rough."

"Whatcha mean?"

"Not waking up to you in my arms. I don't know how I'll ever sleep again." I shake my head and smile.

"I'm sure you'll figure out something." I smirk.

"Yeah, it's called sneaking into your bedroom window after Mr. Lowery has gone to bed."

"Uh, I don't think so. He'd kill us both."

As he approaches me, he takes the shirt from my hand

and throws it onto the top of the bag. He takes one arm and pulls me in to him before placing his forehead on mine. "Raegan, I know that would never work with him, but it was worth a try. I hope you know how much you mean to me." I smile in agreement. "Also, know you're never walkin' outta my life again."

"I don't want to," I say as I meet his eyes.

"Good." He kisses me like his life depends on it. "Come on. Let me help you finish. You know they're waitin' on us," he says. *How is it that guys can pack in one bag?* We finish packing my things and then head to Cole's truck. As we drive down the driveway toward the main road, I glance over my shoulder and see the top of the house. Oh, how I wish I could stay in that bubble.

Emmett

As we drive down the road, it is very evident that Raegan has something on her mind. What, I'm not sure, but I don't say anything to her. Instead, I wrap my arm around her shoulder and kiss the top of her head. Cole and Tammy begin to have a war over radio stations, and as soon as I hear *her* song, I put a stop to it.

"Cole, leave it right there," I say as Raegan looks up to me and smiles. "Are you gonna sing it for us or what?" I ask her.

"Maybe with a little help from you." She winks. *Gosh, I freakin' love this girl.* As she begins to sing, I jump in there with her. Cole and Tammy look at us like we have totally lost it, but it's not until the chorus that I realize how this song is exactly how I feel about Raegan Lowery. Two nights of her in my favorite t-shirt reaching over me has done me in, and I wouldn't trade it for a million bucks. As the song ends, she leans up and kisses my lips. We are brought back to reality when Cole tells us he can get us a room.

CHAPTER 36

Raegan

When we arrive back at the farm, Emmett helps me with my bags as we go into the house. "Grandaddy, I'm home!" I holler as I shut the door. Emmett takes my bag to my room as I walk through the house looking for Grandaddy. *He's nowhere. That's strange.* "Grandaddy!" I yell a little louder. After I search the entire house, I look to make sure his truck is parked outside. *It is.* My heart begins to race. I check the back porch. *Nope.* Hurrying back inside, I run smack into Emmett's chest. "I don't know where he is," I state with fear teetering in my voice.

He wraps his arms around me. "Rae, it's okay. He's 'round here somewhere." We walk outside to meet Cole, and he must notice the fear in my eyes because he jumps out of the truck and runs toward me.

"Cole, I don't know where he is! He's not in the house or on the back porch." Cole's eyes begin to scan the perimeter, and he notices the door to the barn is ajar. He points, and I take off running with Cole and Emmett hot on my tracks. "Grandaddy!" I yell once again as I open the door, but I'm not prepared for what is before me. Grandaddy is stooped over and barely catching his breath. I rush to his side. "What's wrong?" I question. He just shakes his head that he's fine, but deep down I know he's not.

"Cole, let's give them a minute," Emmett says, and they exit the barn.

"Grandaddy, what's wrong?" I ask as tears threaten my eyes.

"I'm fine, Sunshine," he says.

I want to know what is going on, but when I look at his legs, I see the obvious. They are swelling. *Oh my gosh. It's back. His cancer is back.* I shake my head no, and he pulls me into his chest. "Please, tell me I'm wrong," I beg. He doesn't say a word. He just lets me cry in his arms, and if I thought the first round was unbearable, there are no words to describe the storm that is brewing inside.

"Sunshine, the leukemia is back." *Oh God, please no! I can't lose him. I won't lose him.* "I've known for some time now, but I didn't want you to worry about me. I'm living my life like I always have, but this time I've chosen a different path." With those words, I know he wants his quality of life, not quantity. Not that I agree with him, because selfishly I want to keep him forever, but for some strange reason, I understand. He is a strong man, one that works from sun up to sun down. He puts the pedal to the metal, doesn't ask for help, and if he can't do those things, then life is not worth living. I don't want him to leave this Earth, but I also don't want him to spend years in a bed helpless. Making this realization is the hardest, but most freeing at the same time.

"Grandaddy, what do you need me to do?" He takes a step back and looks at me.

"Nothin', I'm living my life to the fullest every day. None of us are guaranteed tomorrow, but if tomorrow doesn't come, then I want to make sure I have nothing left to regret."

"I'm here to help make that happen. What's first?"

"Sunshine, nothing's changing, but first thing tomorrow, I'm goin' shoppin'!" He cackles.

"For what?" I'm also scared to know what he's talking about.

"'Round the corner. I don't want you have to worry about what I might want when I'm gone. So, I'm going to take care of it for ya." *Holy cow, he's going funeral shopping! Are you kidding me?!*

"Do you want me to go with ya?"

"Nah, Cole can. You need to go to school."

"Okay," I say, and I'm truly unsure of how I feel about him shopping for his own funeral. It's kind of morbid when you think about it.

Emmett

As Cole and I wait for Raegan and Mr. Lowery to finish their discussion, he looks at me.

"You know she's about to go ballistic." I say.

"Yeah, like a tornado coming straight toward me." And, that's the only way to put it, because I know it will hurt her, but it's a minor detail in the grand scheme of things.

"I guess it's now or never, Cole. I know we promised we'd talk to her about it, I just didn't think it would be as soon as we got back."

"I know, but she has to know we're here for her." I nod in agreement as we quietly step back into the barn.

CHAPTER 37

Raegan

"Does Cole know?" I ask Grandaddy.

"Yes, he knows things are changing, and so does Emmett." *Wait. What did he say? He knew and didn't tell me? Oh, heck no!*

"What do you mean Emmett knew?" My voice rises.

"Sunshine, calm down. I wanted to tell you, but I wanted you to live your life without worry. I also knew you would push Emmett away if I told you, and I will not let you do that again. He loves you. I need to know he's in your life when I'm no longer here. That's why he knows. Please, don't be mad at him. If you're gonna be upset with someone, be upset with me."

Trying my best to choose my words carefully, I toss that thought out the window and let my lips move. "Mad? I'm freakin' pissed! How could y'all? I love *all* of you! You kept this away from me for what? Me to have some fun? Seriously?!" I say as I start to storm out of the barn but realize it's no use when Cole and Emmett block me from leaving.

Looking at both of them, I step toward them, and they look like they are watching a ghost. "I'm pissed, but he's what's important right now, not either of you. I will not give in to what my head is telling me to do, but I also will not be lied to." *Guess that's kinda funny since I've lied about Grandaddy for months before. I guess what comes around goes around.* "Boys, I love you both, but that man over there, he's my world. And, if this is the end of the road for him, y'all are gonna have to man up and do what needs to be done, no questions asked."

Cole and Emmett look at each other. "We're not going *anywhere*, Rae," Emmett says, and Cole agrees. "So, that's it, Rae? You're not going to push me away?"

"No, but just remember, you're not the focus right now. Grandaddy is."

"I understand. What do we need to do?" Emmett replies.

"I have no idea. I guess we need to ask him." With that, we look toward Grandaddy. I walk toward him and hug him. As I tell him I'm sorry for my behavior, I feel two sets of arms engulf us both. At this point, I know that the four of us are in it for the long haul. We are in this together—Grandaddy, Cole, Emmett, and I. We spend the next hour discussing what will happen over the next month or so. I've now learned Grandaddy's future and how it will affect his body. After supper, Cole and Emmett go home, and I make sure to let Emmett know my feelings for him haven't changed. Lighting up the screen, I send him a text explaining exactly how I feel.

As Monday begins a new week, it begins a new way of life for each of us. Emmett and I go to school while Cole and Grandaddy work on the farm. After school, we both hurry over to help out any way we can, and we repeat this routine each day. When the weekends arrive, I do most of the work. I even let Jordyn in on the secret. She cries forever when she learns the news, and then she gets pissed, because I kept all of it from her for so long. Eventually, she gets over it and begins to help on

Saturdays. Of course, she brings Ridge along because she isn't going to get too dirty. On Sundays, we attend church and relax.

Now, after about two weeks, things have begun to change. Grandaddy's legs have swollen more, so walking has become tough. Getting in and out of the truck is almost impossible. He isn't willing to give up driving, but he knows he has to for everyone's safety. I think that is actually worse than the cancer. Men and their pride, I will never understand. On Sunday, I drive us to church. I have to help him lift his legs into my truck, but we make it. Several people ask if everything is okay, and of course, Grandaddy brushes it off like it is no big deal. He won't let people see him weak. He wants their memory of him to be one of honor and strength.

Sunday night, I begin to panic because I don't want to leave him alone. *Who needs school?* I know Cole will be here, but he's working. They both assure me that Cole won't leave him alone. Plus, Grandaddy is still trying to work as much as he can tolerate, even though there is a major difference in the amount of work he is able to do.

Monday morning I get up, take care of my chores on the farm, and when I walk back into the house, I can't help but smile as I see Grandaddy cooking our breakfast just like he would do any other day, except this morning he is using a cane to balance.

"I'm gonna go change real quick. Are you good?" I ask.

"Lordy, I'm fine! Just hurry before you're late for school." I laugh on my way up the stairs. I shower, dress, and make my way back downstairs. That's when I hear the sounds of pots and pans hitting the wooden floor, or at least that's what I think I hear. I drop my backpack and run downstairs to discover Grandaddy on the floor.

"Oh my gosh! Are you okay?" I say as I kneel next to

him.

"I'm fine. It's just these legs. They don't want to work anymore." When I look down, I see his ankles bulging over his shoes, and it hurts my heart to know he's suffering. He insists I go on to school. Once Cole arrives, he walks me to the truck.

"Rae, we might have to call someone in to help if he gets worse." I shake my head no.

"I'll stay home if I need to," I tell him.

"Oh, yeah, that's gonna fly with him."

"I know he won't let me, but I will not stay at school worrying." Cole and I bicker back and forth for a few minutes before Grandaddy walks out on the porch and hollers for me to go on. I run back to the porch and hug him before going to school.

Emmett

As I'm waiting on Raegan in the parking lot, my phone rings, and it's Cole.

"What's up?" I ask.

"Listen, Uncle Dover fell this mornin'. He made Rae go to school, but I have a feeling things are about to go downhill fast. Just be ready, because she's going to need you."

"Has he been back to the doctor?"

"Actually, Dr. Charles is coming here today. He didn't tell Rae, but they are calling in Hospice." *How am I going to keep this from her?* Just as I begin to question what I am going to do, I see her pulling into the parking lot.

"Okay, well, she just pulled up. Keep me posted. I'll help out any way I can." We hang up, and I hurry to meet her. I open my arms to embrace her, and she stops.

"You've talked to Cole. Haven't you, Em?"

"Yup, what can I do?" I ask.

"Just be there. I have a feelin' my life is 'bout to change."

"I believe you're right, and I'm not leavin' your side." I don't tell her what Cole told me, but I let her know I'm here for her no matter what.

CHAPTER 38

Raegan

After school, Emmett follows me to the house along with Jordyn. *I'm not sure why she insisted on coming, but whatever.* As soon as I walk inside, I now know. This is the end for Grandaddy. I see him in his recliner with a cup of ice water on the side table.

"Hey, Sunshine. Tell me 'bout your day."

"Ah, ya know, same old stuff just a different day. How 'bout you tell me 'bout yours?"

Cole is sitting on the couch. "Come on, y'all. Let's give them a minute," he says to Jordyn and Emmett.

"Sunshine, Dr. Charles came to visit me today. They are calling in Hospice." I nod my head to let him know I understand as tears stream from my eyes.

"How long?" I whisper.

"They don't know. I just want to have everything in place for when it gets bad."

"Okay, what do I need to do?" I question.

"Nothin', you do enough already. I couldn't ask for a better girl than you. I've been blessed to be your grandaddy, and I've lived a great life. I do hate that I'm gonna miss you graduating and your wedding, but I'll be looking down from above with your mama, daddy, and mawmaw."

"How do you know you won't make it that long?" I cry.

"I don't, but I want you to be prepared." I nod. "Come here. You know you don't have to put on that act for me."

"Yes, I do." I say as tears begin to fill my eyes.

"Why do you feel that way, Sunshine?"

"Because of the funeral."

Grandaddy looks at me with a confused look. "What do you mean? The funeral?"

"Remember how I couldn't get those stupid shoes to buckle, and you helped me?" He smiles remembering. "You told me to be extra good, and from that day forward I did as you asked."

"Oh, Sunshine! I never meant for you to take it that way. I'm so sorry. You were always a good girl. I'm so sorry you took that to heart. I love you, Sunshine, and you are perfect just being the Raegan Lowery that God made."

As tears continue to spill, I hug him and don't let go, because I don't know how many more hugs I'm going to be granted with this man. I just don't know how I'll survive my future without him, and then I look up to see Cole, Jordyn, and Emmett. I now know how I will survive. I will survive because I have people that love me.

As I stand, they all embrace me in a hug. "We aren't going anywhere, Rae. We love you both too much," Jordyn says as we all cry in each other's arms. Grandaddy chimes in.

"Quit all that cryin'. I ain't dead yet!" I laugh as I wipe the salty tears from my face. "And, there better not be any cryin' when I'm gone either. Y'all understand that?" he says as he looks at us.

"Yes, sir," Cole and Emmett say.

"I'm not making a promise I can't keep," Jordyn replies, and I agree with her.

When Grandaddy is tired of us crying and moping, he turns on the TV to any game he can find. That makes me realize he's probably never gonna get to see the Braves play live, and it breaks my heart. That's one promise I'll keep for him. We're going to that game.

Emmett

Watching Mr. Lowery tell Raegan breaks my heart. I want to hold them both in my arms and tell them it will be okay, but we all know that it will not be. All I can do is be there for her. Jordyn heads home, and Raegan excuses herself for a few minutes.

In these few minutes, Mr. Lowery wastes no time.

"Boys, I know this going to be hard on each of you, not just Sunshine, but I need you to know what I expect from each of you." He tells us exactly how he expects her future to go, what roles Cole and I will play, and what he has planned for her after he passes. It amazes me that a man who is in his final days can still have a positive outlook on life, but I also know he wants the best for his Sunshine. No matter what I have to do, I'm going to make sure his Sunshine gets everything he ever wished for her.

CHAPTER 39

Raegan

I'm not really sure why I leave them alone, but I do. I almost feel like Grandaddy wants to talk to them about me or maybe them. I don't know, but all I know is I go to my room, grab that bunny and pray like I never have before. I pray that God won't let Grandaddy suffer, that He will take him before that happens, and that he knows I'll be okay. As tears stream down my face, I hear that all too familiar voice of my mama, as well as her touch on my skin. In that moment, she whispers into my ear it is going to be okay, and by being his Sunshine, I'll continue to shine brightly for the entire world to see. Then, as quickly as she came, she is gone. I dry my tears, touch up my makeup, and head back downstairs to see Emmett, Cole, and Grandaddy yelling at the TV as the official makes some lame call, and I know in my heart, this life is good no matter what it might throw my way.

Cole and Emmett eat supper with us and Grandaddy explains a few things to us.

"Raegan, we need to talk about a few things, and I want the boys to be here. Are you okay with that?" He questions.

"Yes, sir."

"Over the past few months I've been meeting with Joe about what I want to happen when I am gone. When your parents passed, I set up a trust fund for you from their life insurance policies, but I don't want you to use that unless you absolutely need to. I want the farm to be your income. Cole has agreed to run the farm with you both being partners, if that's okay with you."

"Grandaddy, this is a lot to take in. Are you sure this is what you want?"

"Sunshine, I've thought this through. Cole and you have worked on this farm and know everything about it. If things continue to prosper, you won't have to ever worry about income. You can still go to college and be a young adult, but this way I know you're taken care of."

I look toward Cole and then to Emmett for their thoughts. "Rae, I love this farm and if this is something you want me to be a part of, I'd be honored." Cole states.

"Grandaddy, this farm is my home. I can't see myself anywhere else. I promise we will make you proud. Isn't that right, Cole?"

"You bet." He says.

Emmett remains pretty quiet throughout the conversation, and I know that he's trying not to overstep his boundaries.

Once the conversation about my future is complete, we finish supper, and Cole lightens the mood with stories about great times we've had. Emmett begins to relax, and as I look around the table, I know that I'm surrounded by people that truly love me for me.

When the table is cleared and the dishes are finished, Cole and Emmett head home. This is when things begin to change. I have to help Grandaddy remove his shoes because his feet are swollen so much, and then I have to walk with him for stability to the restroom. Honestly, it is for me to make sure he is okay. By Tuesday morning, I know his days are numbered. Grandaddy insists I go to school, but my mind can't focus. On Thursday, I see the guidance counselor and inform her of Grandaddy's situation. I know confidentiality is big in her department; therefore, I feel comfortable talking to her. Of course, she offers all types of counseling, but I'm not interested.

Each day is the same routine for me. I get up, check on Grandaddy, check on the farm, and then help him slide on his shoes, until today. They won't fit, and I see the defeat in his eyes. "Get my slippers," he says. I do as he says and make my way to school.

Our weekend is spent with Grandaddy, and he's doing a lot of resting at this point. He's still stubborn as a mule and independent, but I know the time is approaching. On Thursday, my fears become my reality when he begins to slip further and further away. I don't go to school and neither does Emmett. He and Cole are right beside me.

After breakfast, Grandaddy asks for us to call the nurse, and I know things must be bad. When Christie arrives, we smile. She's as sweet as sugar, and Grandaddy loves her. For the longest time, when she'd come to check on him, he'd try to push her out the door so she could visit all the people worse than him.

"Rae, how is he?" she asks me.

"Not good," I say as a sob escapes. "But, he's still acting like nothing is wrong with him." She laughs and makes her way to check on him. When she finishes, she comes back out and gives me the information I knew was coming.

"It could be anytime now. I'll be back later today to

check on him."

"Thank you for everything," I say in appreciation.

Once I go back to check on him, I see his breath is becoming more labored. I know I will not go to school tomorrow because he is more important, no matter what he tells me.

We have a rough night. Cole stays with me, and we take turns staying up while Grandaddy sleeps. Hank hasn't left Grandaddy's side since he permanently moved to his bedroom, and he knows that something is going on.

As the sun rises, Grandaddy begins to mumble something about fishing, and I try not to giggle. Then, the reality sets in that this is the end. "Grandaddy, I'm here," I say as I take his hand.

When he wakes up, he looks at me. "I'm so tired, Sunshine. I'm so tired. Why won't the good Lord take me home?" he says.

I have no idea what to say, and then out of thin air, the words roll off my tongue. "Grandaddy, maybe there's a line to get in today, and God wants you to stay with me here so you don't have to stand and wait."

A smile escapes his lips. "Maybe you're right, Sunshine, but, oh, I'm *so* tired." He begins to cough, and I call for Cole. He runs into the room.

"Go call Christie," he tells me. I race to call her, but as I do, I begin to break as I lose *my* Sunshine. He's always been the light in my life. What am I going to do without him?

"Christie, we need you," I manage to say.

"I'm on my way," she responds as the phone disconnects.

After hanging up the phone, I rush back to Grandaddy's side. Cole and I talk to him like it's a normal day. He gets out of bed to use the restroom and even posts himself on the edge of the bed as we wait for Christie.

Within twenty minutes, there is a knock on the door. "Mornin,' Mr. Lowery. How are we doin' today?" she asks as she moves to take a seat beside him on the bed.

He looks at her. "I could be better, I guess." Then, he laughs, and we all laugh. Even when the light is dim, he continues to be positive.

After Christie assesses the situation, she goes to the refrigerator. "Mr. Lowery, I'm gonna give you some medicine to make you comfortable. Just enough to help you rest a little." He looks at me, and I nod my head. She proceeds to give him a dose of morphine. Seeing him take that medicine, I know it's needed, and within twenty minutes, he is resting peacefully.

I take a step out into the hallway toward the kitchen to see Christie waiting. "I thought you had left?" I ask.

"No, Rae, I just wanted to make sure he got to sleep. How are you?"

"Hard to believe, but right now, I'm okay. As much as it hurts to lose him, I don't want him to suffer. I know it could be worse, but my heart can't take it," I say as I sit at the kitchen table with her.

"I understand. I want you to know I'm here if you ever need me, even after all of this is over," she says as she takes my hands in hers. "That grandaddy of yours is special. I've never met anyone like him. It's always been more about conversation and friendship than being his nurse. He wouldn't have it any other way."

"I know. I was worried in the beginning, because he doesn't let anyone know his business, but you came in, and he was okay with it. I'm glad you were the one sent to us."

"Me, too," she replies. "I'm going to make a few more

calls. If you need me, call me. I will check back in later today."

"Yes, ma'am," I say, walking her to the door before going back to Grandaddy's side. "Cole, you can go home for a while if you want, or go check on the farm. Don't feel like you have to stay here all day," I state.

"Raegan, I can't believe you'd say that. I love that man more than you know, but if you are okay for a few minutes, I'm going to feed the animals in the barn and check the water. Emmett's coming around lunch."

"Good, and that's fine. I haven't checked the chicken house either, and Cole, I didn't mean to be that harsh a second ago. My emotions are runnin' crazy."

Cole walks over to me and holds me tightly. "There's no need to apologize. I feel the same way. I'll be back in a few minutes."

He exits the room, and I sit beside Grandaddy in the chair next to his bed. I watch as he sleeps peacefully, but his breathing is hard and a big puff escapes when he exhales. As he sleeps, I say what is on my heart, "It's okay, Grandaddy. I'm going to be fine. You don't have to hold on any longer, and no matter what, I'll never let you go."

In his sleep, he mutters, "I'll never let you go, Sunshine, but I'm wore slap out."

"I know you are. Rest a while until the line's an express lane." I slide out of my chair and onto the floor beside the bed. I continue to hold his hand as I rest my head on the edge of his bed. Before I realize it, the sounds of voices wake me. Cole and Emmett have slipped into the room.

"Have a nice snooze there?" Cole asks, and panic sets in as I look at Grandaddy to see if he's still breathing. His breaths are further apart, but he's resting. "You think we need to call Christie?" he asks. I just shake my head no.

"I just want the four of us in this room when the time comes."

"Are you sure?" he asks once more.

"I'm sure," I reply and neither says another word. Cole takes my seat in the chair as I sit on the bed with Grandaddy, and Emmett stands to the side. Grandaddy's eyes open, and a smile crosses his face when he looks at me. "Grandaddy, you want me to sing for ya?"

"That'd be perfect, Sunshine." Just like that, I look at him and smile as I begin to sing his favorite hymn, "Amazing Grace". Grandaddy does his best to sing with me, but by the final verse, he doesn't say a word. He smiles at me, and mouths he loves me. Tears begin to flood my eyes, and I give him everything I have. As I sing the final note, he takes his last breath.

As the reality sets in, I scan the room to find Cole and Emmett. Cole looks at his watch for Grandaddy's time of death as Emmett moves toward me, and all I can do is hold onto Grandaddy. His hand is warm as I cry for him and what my life will be like without him. Emmett embraces me from behind, and I sob. Vaguely, I can hear Cole on the phone with someone whom I assume is Christie, but I can only focus on the body in front of me.

Emmett loosens his grip on me, and I crawl into bed with Grandaddy and hug him, just like he did me all those years ago when I lost almost everyone that was important to me.

Emmett

As we walk outside, Cole gets choked up, but pushes the tears behind him. "Cole, it's okay to cry. He's like another dad to you."

"I know, but I promised not to cry. He wouldn't want it that way," he says as Christie's car pulls up the driveway.

She doesn't knock. She just comes inside and looks at us before making her way to Mr. Lowery's room.

"Cole, this is a new beginning for all of us. We need to be there for Rae, but we also need to be there for each other. You're the best brother I could have asked for, and I'm here for ya. Just like I know you're going to be here for me."

"You know I'll be here for ya. I just hope that when Uncle Dover looks down on us, we make him proud in everything we do. I want his legacy in this town to live on, and we can do that keeping up the farm and running it like Uncle Dover did. I hope one day, I'm half the man he was."

CHAPTER 40

Raegan

As I lie there holding my grandaddy, I hear the door creak open. I keep my eyes closed and try to hold on to the peace I've had for the past few minutes. Those moments where it's just he and I alone in his room. Then, I feel the bed sag as someone sits.

"Raegan, it's Christie. The funeral home people are on their way. Are you going to be okay being in here for this?" she asks gently.

"Yes, I'm not leaving him." With that, I hold him for a little while longer until they arrive, and then I watch as they place him onto a gurney and roll him through the house. As they make their way out the front door and off the porch, I notice Hank following them. "Hank, come here, boy," I say. He stops to look at me, but continues to follow them. I step toward the door when Emmett stops me. "I've got to get him." He nods, and I walk out the door toward Hank. "Come here, boy," I repeat as I approach him. I squat down to his level and scratch him behind the ear. "Hank, he's gone, buddy." I can see the sadness in his eyes. "I know. I'm sad, too, but he's with Mama,

Daddy, and Mawmaw. It's just you and me from now on," I say and wait for his reaction. He tilts his head to the side and grins at me. Inside, I know he understands exactly what I said, and as the van drives out the driveway, we both stand and watch as Grandaddy leaves the Lowery farm for the last time.

When we can no longer see him, I cry uncontrollably, and Hank brushes up against me. I bend down to him and cry until Emmett scoops me up and takes me inside, as Hank trails behind us.

I have no idea what time it is when I wake up, but I feel an emptiness in my soul. *Grandaddy is gone.* I look to my right and see Emmett at the other end of the couch. When he realizes I'm awake, he smiles my way.

"Hey, Sleepin' Beauty," he says, and I smile back.

"Why'd y'all let me sleep like that?"

"You needed it. It's only been a few hours, and everything is taken care of for now."

"I'm sure I need to do something," I say as I sit up.

"No, you don't. The pastor will be by after supper, Mama has supper on the way, and Cole has gone home to shower and sleep for a little while. I'm not going anywhere."

Instead of speaking, I just slide into his arms and don't say another word. We sit like that until there is a knock on the door. He rises to get it, and I wait to see whom it is. I soon realize it's the beginning of the never-ending food committee. I know I should be thankful, but it's just me for crying out loud. I've never understood why people want to bring so much food anyway. *Oh, well.* I stand and put on a happy face to greet them and continue to do the same until George and Emma arrive. At this point, she takes over, and once we eat supper, I wait for our pastor.

The remainder of the night, we discuss what service

Grandaddy wants, and I pull out the book from the safe. It has every detail of the funeral and then our pastor begins to ask about memories. At this point, I'm not sure if I can handle it, but thinking of all our good times makes me forget that he's gone.

"Hey, Rae, do you remember that time when you refused to collect eggs because you said you weren't gonna be a baby bird killer, and that he should just buy them at the grocery store?" Cole asks.

"Uh, yeah, Grandaddy enlightened me on how they ended up in the store, and needless to say, from that day forward, I never bucked what he wanted me to do," I say. "Cole, do you remember that time he caught you with that case of beer?" I giggle and cover my mouth.

Cole looks at me like he could kill me, and then I realize his dad is here. "Yeah, he made me start pouring all of them out, but then changed his mind because that was being wasteful. He called his buddy Joe, and I had to give them to him. The sad part was, I'd worked so hard to find a way to buy them. I thought I was so slick." He shakes his head. "But, my favorite is when he talked about the war. Y'all know how he got that gun right there?" We all shake our head. "He traded liquor for it. He loved to tell me those stories when we'd come inside for lunch."

After those stories, we get serious and talk about things that could be spoken about in the service. He was always singing, working hard, and on the tractor. Everyone knew who he was in the town, and they all admired his work ethic. Most of all, they loved how much he loved the Lord, even with the cards he was dealt twelve years ago. No matter what, he always spoke the truth, even if it hurt someone's feelings, and he never gave up. Even today, he never gave up; he knew it was time to move on, and move on, he did.

As the pastor leaves, George and Emma insist I come to their house, but I refuse. I don't want to leave. This is my home. I look at Cole and Emmett, and they both know what I'm thinking. They aren't leaving either. Once George and Emma leave, we all decide to call it a night. Cole sleeps in the guest room, and Emmett sleeps with me.

"Do you think he's gonna strike me dead?" Emmett asks as he holds me close.

"Nah, he might be turning his head, though." Emmett holds me tighter and kisses my cheek as I cry myself to sleep in his arms.

The next day is full with meeting with the men in suits and making sure everything is in line for the service tomorrow. Grandaddy had chosen to have a service at our church and then visitation afterward in the fellowship hall. He wanted a celebration, and that's what he was going to get.

As the day of the service approaches, I do my best to hold myself together, but this is making it real. This is the day I have to say goodbye. Cole and Emmett have gone home to shower and get dressed. Honestly, I just wanted a little time alone. As the minutes pass by, I begin to regret my decision to be alone. The deep sadness I feel for not having Grandaddy begins to consume me. I push it to the side, as I get ready. Looking in my closet, I find a black A-line dress with silver embellishments on the neckline, and as I go to grab it from the closet, I change my mind when I see a bright yellow dress. *That's what he would want.* I take it and slide it on with the perfect boots. As I apply my makeup and style my hair, I break down as I look in the mirror, but stop myself. *I can be strong for him, just like when I was five.* I wipe away the tears and apply my makeup yet again and hear a knock on the door.

"Come in," I say as I apply my lipstick. I see Emmett standing there in a charcoal gray suit with his hair perfectly styled, and I smile at him.

"Are you 'bout ready?" he questions.

"As much as I'll ever be," I say as I make my way to him, and he holds me in his arms. I pull away before the tears start again.

As we walk downstairs, Joe, Emma, George, Cole, and a few distant relatives greet us. We make our way to our cars and caravan to the church.

As time approaches, we line up to enter. When we begin to walk inside, I turn to Emmett. "I can't do this." I begin to cry and shake my head no.

"Yes, you can," he says as he clutches me by the arm while Cole takes my other side. We make our way down front and celebrate the life of my grandaddy, Dover Lowery. We laugh, cry, and when it comes time, I leave the pew, and keep my promise to him. I sing "Amazing Grace" the way he loved to hear it, and as I close my eyes, I can hear him harmonizing with me that last time. A tear streams down my face, but not before a smile escapes my lips.

When the song ends, I take my seat and listen to the pastor say a few last words. As the pallbearers carry him out, we exit behind them and then make our way to the fellowship hall. I'm in awe as I see how much people love us in this town. Instead of your typical visitation, there is a meal with plenty of fellowship. It honestly reminds me of a homecoming celebration. *Homecoming. That's what happened, isn't it? He went home.*

This time the men in suits aren't a threat, because rather than being scared of the unknown or going to say goodbye, we are laughing, reminiscing, and celebrating the life of a man that called me Sunshine.

Emmett

Watching everyone celebrate the life of Mr. Lowery brings a light into my heart. He not only was he the love of my life's grandaddy, but he was a man that I've grown to respect. He never worried about the cards he was dealt, but instead, he took life by the horns and lived it to the fullest.

As the crowd begins to diminish from the fellowship hall, I move in closer to Raegan. It's almost as if she senses what is about to happen and she holds onto me for dear life.

"Raegan, are you ready?" I ask as the last person leaves. She clutches my arms tighter. "As I'll ever be." She says. I kiss the top of her forehead and we make our way to the door with Cole, my mom, and George.

As we drive closer and closer to the farm, I see the tears begin to stream down Raegan's face. Not knowing what I can do or should do to make her smile, I decide it's time to take her to a happier place and time. I take the first road once we reach the property line and turn toward the creek. Raegan looks toward me and smiles as tears fall from her face, but as I plug in my iPhone into the radio adapter and begin to play, "That's Where It's At," she grins as if she knows what is about to happen. I walk around the truck, take her by the hand, and we dance by the water. In this moment, I know that her entire family is watching, and I don't want them to turn their head. I want them to know that I'm taking care of their girl, in this moment and forevermore.

EPILOGUE

Four Months Later

Raegan

After waking up to the sound of the rooster, I make my way downstairs and begin working on the farm. Over the past four months, my life has changed dramatically. I'm no longer keeping up with appearances; I now wear my emotions on my sleeves and say what I am thinking. I'm still the girl that everyone loves at Cleveland High, but I no longer worry about what others think.

"Hey, Cole," I say as I turn on the coffee pot. After Grandaddy's passing, Cole moved in. He's made a permanent residence here with me. I just don't want to be alone, and Emmett is not an option because his mother isn't having it. Plus, it's not right, and Grandaddy would roll over in his grave.

"Mornin', Rae, are you ready for this weekend?" he asks.

"You bet! I've been waiting on it forever," I say with excitement.

"Oh, there's something for you on the table from Joe." I walk to the kitchen table and see an off white envelope from

Joe's office. *Probably some more legal stuff to take care of.* I open it immediately and freeze when I recognize the handwriting. *Grandaddy.* I look up to Cole, and he smiles as a whirlwind of emotions begin to attack my body. He walks out of the room, and I take a seat to read it.

Dear Sunshine,

If you're reading this, I didn't make it. I'm sorry. I didn't want to leave you alone, and I can honestly say that when I left this world, you weren't alone. You have a support system that loves you.

When I had to take those treatments, I knew it wasn't going to end well. I talked to both Cole and Emmett and asked them to keep it from you. I had my reasons. Most importantly, I wanted to spend my days with you enjoying life and not worrying about me. I wanted to see you living. Secondly, I wanted to see how Cole and Emmett would handle the task I had given them. They both succeeded. I'm thankful to have had them in my life as well as yours.

Sunshine, I'm going to miss some important events in your life. From this point on, if you need parental advice, talk to George and Emma, and when Emmett does something stupid, have Cole handle it. I'll look down on it and laugh from Heaven.

Emmett, now, he's a catch. We had many a talk without you knowing. Actually Cole and him. He loves you with everything he can give, and one day he's gonna ask you to be his wife. Don't act like you didn't know this already, but act totally shocked when it does happen. When he does, he has my permission. I've already told him personally.

When I think about you getting married, I hate I won't be there to walk you down the aisle, but Cole will be. He is to give you away, and on that day, as well as every other, I'll be looking down on you, Sunshine! Don't ever let that light fade. I love you with everything I have to give.

Love,
Grandaddy

I sit as the tears fall, and then Cole comes to stand beside me. I look up at him and stand and wrap my arms around him. "Thank you for always being there, Cole. I love you," I say mid-cry, and he begins to cry as well.

"I love you, too. Just so you know, it would be an honor to give you away one of these days." I smile as I place the note into my back pocket.

Within the hour, we are packing the truck and making our way to Atlanta. As we enter the city, all the big buildings and insane traffic amaze me. I can almost hear Grandaddy fussing the entire way. We check into the hotel and then walk around before supper.

As Emmett and I walk hand in hand, we pass a tattoo parlor. I stop and look at him.

"Are you kidding me?" he asks.

"No." He looks confused, but follows me inside.

"Are you sure?" Emmett questions.

"More than anything in my life. I want to keep him near me," I say as I pull the note from my back pocket.

We walk inside, and within the hour, I have the most beautiful signature on my left wrist. *Love, Grandaddy.* A permanent ink for a man who has a permanent place in my heart. I'm surprised at how the pain felt like it was healing my grieving heart. Emmett looks at it and smiles.

"It's perfect, but you know he's fussing for you doin' that to your body, right?" he says.

"Yeah, well, I want him always, and this keeps him with me forever." Emmett and I walk from the tattoo parlor and meet up with Cole, Tammy, Jordyn and Ridge. They quickly notice the plastic wrap on my wrist, and Cole's eyes fill with tears when he sees the handwritten signature.

"Rae, he might be fussing right now, but deep down, he's in love with it," Cole says.

We enjoy supper at Hard Rock Café and then head back to the hotel to get ready for the game tomorrow.

The next morning, as we get ready to walk to Turner Field to see the Atlanta Braves play the Boston Redsox, I grab Grandaddy's old Braves cap and put it on. My heart is heavy, knowing Grandaddy never got to witness a game live, but as we take our seats and I stare down at the ink on my left wrist, I know he's with me. From this day forward, he continues to live through me. I will forever be his Sunshine, and I'm a better person because he shared his life with me.

As the speakers begin to play "Kiss Me," and the camera scans the crowd for couples, I watch the jumbotron to see where the camera is going to go. I love to see how people react, but I pray it doesn't land on us. I'm not so sure I want to make out in front of thousands of people.

As the song begins to evaporate into the air, the camera stops on me. I realize Em isn't beside me. *What in the world?* When I glance to his seat, I see him on one knee with a ring that is oh so familiar, my mama's. My hand covers my mouth as I start to cry uncontrollably.

"Raegan Lowery, when we were kids, I knew you were special, but each and every day you amaze me more. You are the light in my day and I know that right now, in this moment, your entire family is looking down on us. Will you please do me the honor of being Mrs. Emmett Bridges?"

As the crowd erupts, I shake my head yes as Emmett stands, places the ring on my shaking left ring finger, and then kisses me for the world to see. Right now, in this moment and forever, Emmett Bridges is where it's at.

A NOTE FROM CASEY PEELER

On my birthday, August 23, 2013, my world was rocked. I lost one of the most influential men in my life, my pawpaw. From the day I was born on August 23, 1981, until the day he passed, August 23, 2013, I believed the sun set in him, just as he did me. See, I was "his girl," but I was also his caregiver in the final days. He has been one of my biggest supporters on this journey as an author, but yet, he didn't get to see me hit *Publish*.

Halfway through the *Full Circle Series*, I knew *Southern Perfection* would have to be written, but honestly, until the words were written on the pages, I never knew the impact it would have on my soul.

Southern Perfection isn't just a good ol' country romance. It's a story of family, taking the good with the bad, always being positive in life regardless the situation, and becoming the person you are destined to become while your loved ones look down and smile upon you each day.

I hope and pray that every one of you that reads this novel has a Sunshine in your life, because even though mine is no longer with me physically, he still continues to shine through me each day.

ABOUT THE AUTHOR

Casey Peeler grew up and still lives in North Carolina with her husband and daughter. Her first passion is teaching students with special needs. Over the years, she found her way to relax was in a good book.

After reading *Their Eyes Were Watching God* by Zora Neal Hurston her senior year of high school and multiple Nicholas Sparks' novels, she found a hidden love and appreciation for reading.

Casey is an avid reader, lifestyle blogger and author. Her perfect day consists of water, sand between her toes, a cold beverage, and a great book!

Come hang with Casey on Social Media
Website- www.authorcaseypeeler.com
Facebook- www.facebook.com/authorcaseypeeler
Instagram- @CaseyPeeler
Pinterest- www.pinterest.com/caseypeeler/
Goodreads-
www.goodreads.com/author/show/7106874.Casey_Peeler

Or join my list by visiting my website to download a FREE copy of Tutus & Cowboy Boots Part 1, and receive a weekly email from me talking about what's up in books, everyday life, and to let me get to know you as a reader too!

www.ingramcontent.com/pod-product-compliance
Lightning Source LLC
Chambersburg PA
CBHW050342030726
47503CB00008B/2567